KEPT BY THE LOAN SHARK

By Roxie Rivera

Night Works Books
3515-B Longmire Drive #103
College Station, Texas 77845
www.roxierivera.com

Publisher's Note: This is a work of fiction. Names, characters, places, and incidents are a product of the author's imagination. Locales and public names are sometimes used for atmospheric purposes. Any resemblance to actual people, living or dead, or to businesses, companies, events, institutions, or locales is completely coincidental.

Cover Art © Katalinks | Dreamstime.com

KEPT BY THE LOAN SHARK/Roxie Rivera—1st ed.

CHAPTER ONE

"YOU SURE YOU'RE too busy to go out tonight?"

I looked up from the papers I was grading to see Taylor standing in the doorway of the office. Her mischievous smile told me she had quite a night planned. "Yep. Hagen is back in town and picking me up."

"Boring," Taylor decreed. "Come out with us instead."

"Us?"

"Kaya and Maddie from the engineering department, June from chemistry, Minh from neuro, Annabelle and LeeAnn from math and, obviously, me—your best friend in the whole world," she added dramatically. "It's a *FRIENDS* themed pub crawl. You love *FRIENDS*," she insisted. "Come out with us!"

"I can barely handle a glass of rosé without getting light-headed. A pub crawl will kill me!"

"You could be our designated driver?" she suggested hopefully.

"Pass." I gave her a thumbs-down at the thought of herding half a dozen drunk friends around downtown Houston.

"Boo!" She stuck out her tongue. "Next time?"

I laughed. "Hard pass."

Taylor rolled her eyes. "Girl, you have got to live a little!" Before I could answer, she held up her hand and said, "Winning the TA *SCRABBLE* tournament doesn't count!"

"Says who?"

"Says everyone who knows how to have fun."

"Hagen thinks I'm fun," I protested.

Her smile turned sly. "Oh, I'm sure he does."

I blushed. "I didn't mean it that way."

Amused, she said, "No, I'm sure you didn't. You're way too sweet to throw your wild sex life with that beast of a man in my face."

"It's not wild," I grumbled, embarrassed. "It's normal. Perfectly normal."

"Uh-huh," she said, unconvinced. "Well, if you change your mind about tonight, call me."

Giving her my full attention so she would know I was serious, I urged, "Be careful, okay? Almost all of the missing girls disappeared after bar hopping."

I expected Taylor to roll her eyes and say something sarcastic, but she actually seemed worried. "That sophomore who went missing three weeks ago?"

"McKenna?"

She nodded. "I saw her at the bar. Danny and I were having a drink, and he noticed her and thought she was cute. I told him to go talk to her, but he was too shy and thought she was too young. It's wild to think we were some of the last people to see her."

"Did you talk to the police?"

"Yeah. We didn't have any details that could help them, but we were able to confirm where she was and when."

Over the last three years, seven young women had gone missing, all of them fellow students. Most were freshman or sophomores, but there had been two grad students among them. All of them had been seen at bars around campus before disappearing. There hadn't been much done to find them, and it was a growing point of contention between university student groups and the police.

"We'll be safe," Taylor promised, knowing full well that I would worry about her. "I'll text you when I get home, okay?"

"Okay, and if you do need a DD, call me."

"I will." She pushed off the door frame and turned to leave. She hesitated and glanced back at me. With a stage whisper, she announced, "Here comes Creeper Kyle."

I glared and hissed, "Don't call him that. He's a nice guy."

"That's what they said about Ted Bundy," she snarked and left.

Hoping Kyle hadn't heard her, I went back to grading. He wasn't a creep. His mannerisms were a bit odd, and he didn't always recognize when he had overstayed his welcome, but he had always been nice to me and a good friend. He even helped me find the apartment where I had lived for the last two years.

"Hey, Cassie!"

"Hey, Kyle." I glanced up from the paper I was grading. "You headed home?"

"Not yet. I have a shift scheduled at the counseling center. What about you?"

"I have a few more of these to grade before I head out."

"Any signs of the next Hawking in that stack?"

I made a face. "I mean, it's only the fourth week of class so..."

"That bad?"

"Yeah."

"Did my notes help with your math lecture?"

"Yes! Thank you so much," I gushed appreciatively. "I was in literal tears trying to figure out what the hell was happening. Your notes made everything so much clearer."

"Good. I'm glad. Don't hesitate to ask for my help. What's the point of having a math nerd living across from you if you can't dig through my old notes?"

Math nerd was his way of being wildly humble. He was four years into his doctorate in mathematics and had won numerous awards throughout his college career. Without his help, I would have struggled to earn a solid B in my tensor and topology courses. I was pretty good at math, but he was truly gifted and a great teacher. Being able to walk a few feet from my apartment to knock on his door and ask for help had been a godsend. I had managed an A in both courses after his tutoring.

"I seriously owe you for talking me down this morning. I was ready to run out of that lecture hall and never come back."

"You're at that point in your education where the math and the concepts just keep getting more complex. You need to believe in yourself more. You're brilliant, Cassie. You have what it takes. I've seen your work."

"Thank you, Kyle. That's really nice for you to say."

"It's the truth. Do you need me to drive you home?"

We had carpooled to the university together that morning. "Hagen is picking me up, but thanks."

"Date night?" he guessed.

"Yes, but super low key. Hagen has been traveling all week so we'll probably do something quiet."

"Not going to meet up with Taylor on their pub crawl?"

"Definitely not," I said with a laugh. "You?"

"Not my scene," he replied and then smiled almost nervously. "I'm taking Hannah to that new vegan restaurant that just opened."

"You asked her out!" I had been encouraging him to ask her on a date. He had met her at a grad student mixer a few weeks ago but had been too shy to shoot his shot. From what I knew of him, Kyle hadn't had much experience dating, but he was so nice that I knew he just had to find the right girl. And he had!

"Yeah." He grinned. "You were right. She was waiting for me to ask."

"See! Sometimes it pays to be bold."

"It sure does." He glanced at his watch. "I should get going. I'll see you around?"

"Yes—and good luck on your date! I want all the details the next time I see you."

After Kyle left, I finished grading the last few exams. I had noticed a theme across more than half of the exams and made a note to the instructor about the physics concepts his students didn't seem to grasp. I made sure the note was succinct, just ten words. Dr. Plotkin wouldn't read a note any longer than that.

I sent a quick text to Hagen, letting him know I was done, and then I delivered the graded papers to Dr. Plotkin's desk, placing them in the correct tray and orienting them so they could be read from his chair. Once that was done, I clocked out, logged off and grabbed my backpack. On my way out of the building, I pulled my phone from the pocket of my jeans and swiped my thumb across the screen.

Hagen: Headed your way

Certain traffic would be hell, I found a shady spot on a bench near our designated pickup area. My gaze drifted to the bulletin board littered with flyers for roommates, used things for sale and MLM opportunities. The tattered, faded flyers for two of the missing women caught my eye.

Like so many fans of crime shows and podcasts, I had done my own sleuthing about the cases, wondering if there was a pattern among the missing girls. Other than being students here, they shared no other similarities. They were different races, heights and builds. Three of them were science students. Two were in liberal arts. The other two were in business and engineering. It would have been less worrying if they had all shared similar looks or interests. At least then we would know why they had been chosen.

If they had been chosen.

The police seemed to believe that most of the missing women had left Houston of their own free will. Some of them were on the verge of failing out of school. A couple of them had just been through horrible breakups.

It was unsettling to think that someone was hunting vulnerable women. Was it another student? A professor? Some random weirdo who had a thing for college-aged girls? Glancing around at the women walking to and from class, I couldn't help but wonder if the next victim was among them. I suddenly had the morbid thought that it might be me.

Shuddering and refusing to give that line of thought another second, I opened Instagram as a distraction. As I scrolled, I enviously eyed the curvy fitness influencers I followed. I had been trying a workout routine that promised a Brazilian butt lift without surgery, but my sad little booty hadn't shown much improvement. My legs looked leaner, more defined, but I hadn't developed the curves I craved. It was hard to embrace my thin, ballerina-like frame when the world seemed to favor lush bombshell figures.

Thankfully, Hagen didn't seem to mind my lack of assets. The few times I had been self-conscious about my small breasts or bottom, he had gone out of his way to show me how much he enjoyed and appreciated those parts of me. He would use his hands and mouth in the wickedest, dirtiest ways until I couldn't even look at him without blushing. When we were together, I felt gorgeous and sexy and completely worthy of his love and adoration.

When I had walked into the back room of his bar to try to save my brother, Ronnie, from a gambling debt, I had never expected to meet a man who would sweep me off my feet. Dark, brooding and big, Hagen was the complete opposite of the men I normally dated. He had taken one look at me and had decided I was meant to be his.

When the black Navigator rolled up to the curb, I tucked away my phone and grabbed my backpack. Looking devastatingly handsome in his crisp white shirt and mirrored aviators, Hagen rolled down the front passenger window and called out, "Hey, sweetheart, I'm lost. You wouldn't happen to have the directions to your heart?"

I rolled my eyes and laughed. He enjoyed teasing me with silly pickup lines, each one worse than the last. "That was awful."

He laughed and leaned across the console to kiss me. He

tasted like sugar and spearmint, the cool after burn of his favorite mints heating my lips. "Buckle up."

After I fastened my seatbelt, he grabbed my backpack and placed it on the floorboard behind us. He made a face, and I knew what was coming. "I'm not replacing it. It's still perfectly good."

"I didn't say anything."

"Your face did."

"Yeah? What's this face saying?"

I lost it when I saw the ridiculous expression he was making. "Stop!"

Still laughing, he merged into traffic and reached across the console to interlace our fingers. Even after all the times he had held my hand, I still marveled at the size differences between us. I barely stood an inch over five feet, and he towered over me by a foot and five inches. We garnered second glances whenever we were out together, but I had stopped noticing most of them. Only Taylor had been bold enough to ask how our height disparity worked in the bedroom, but I was certain she wasn't the only one who wondered.

"How was your day?"

"I had a moment in my math class when I wanted to cry, but other than that, it was fine."

"What? Why? Was your professor an asshole again?" His protective instincts flared, and it made my insides melt.

"No, it was a topology concept that gave me a headache, but Kyle came through with a much easier to follow explanation that helped me nail it."

"Kyle saved the day, huh?"

"Hagen," I sighed, "you know he's just a friend."

"Does he know that? Because I've seen the way he looks at you—"

"He's dating someone," I cut in.

"Is she real?"

"Be nice!" I swatted his muscular thigh. "I don't know why you dislike him so much."

"I don't trust him." He rubbed his thumb over mine in that gentle, soothing way I had come to crave. "I know the type. He's got ulterior motives."

"Like you didn't have ulterior motives when you met me?"

"That was different," he said, ignoring my pointed stare. "So—dinner?"

"Smooth." I shook my head in amusement and decided not to needle him about it. Certain he was worn out from all of his flights and hotel stays, I offered to cook. "I can make dinner."

He hesitated. "You sure? We can go out to eat."

"I enjoy cooking, and I really enjoy cooking for you."

"You spoil me, Cass."

"Not nearly enough," I said, thinking of how much he had done for me and my brother. Hagen never brought up the money he had spent to clear my brother's debts. He never made me feel as though I owed him, and I was grateful for that. Still, I liked showing him how much he meant to me, even through simple domestic acts like making dinner.

"I missed you," Hagen said, his deep, rumbling voice serious. "I don't..." He faltered. "It's never been like this for me. Feeling empty and off kilter when you aren't around," he explained.

"I understand," I assured him. He wasn't the most emotionally open man, and I wanted to encourage him to share thoughts like these again. "It was the same for me. I forgot what it's like to be lonely at night."

He lifted our entwined hands and kissed the back of mine. "You sure as hell won't be lonely tonight."

Heat crept into my face, and I swallowed hard, already imagining all the wicked ways he would keep me company.

CHAPTER TWO

"**C**ASS, I'LL GET those."

"It's fine," I said and shooed him away from the dishwasher. The simple dinner I had pulled together hadn't left many dirty dishes to handle.

"You cooked. The least I can do is put the dishes in the dishwasher," he insisted and manhandled me right out of the way, lifting me up and setting me on the counter. "Sit. Hold this."

Taking the still cold bottle of beer from his hand, I watched as he rinsed and loaded the dishes. Thinking of our earlier dinner conversation about his out of town meetings, I asked, "So—what did you decide? Do you want to invest in one of the firms you visited?"

"I'm not sure," he admitted, swiping the bottle from me and taking a sip. When he handed it back, he said, "I know that I have enough money—legitimate money—to invest with one of the major players, but it's hard to think about putting everything I worked for in someone else's hands."

I ran my thumb along the cold condensation on the neck of the bottle and considered his problem. "So, it's about trust? About putting your savings with a firm you can trust? With people you can trust?"

"Yes." He grabbed a dishwasher pod from under the sink, tossed it in and closed the door. "I thought visiting the offices in San Francisco and New York would put my mind at ease. I know that I was lucky to even get meetings with them."

"*They* were lucky to have *your* interest." He didn't walk around flaunting his wealth. I had been shocked when he had shown me the true amount he had amassed. He seemed to have known from the beginning that his illicit loan sharking would only take him so far. He had been investing his clean money in businesses, real estate and the markets until he had acquired enough that he needed professional expertise.

He grinned and leaned into me, gripping the counter on either side of me. He teased his mouth over mine. "You're good for my ego."

I snorted indelicately and kissed him back. "Your ego doesn't need my help."

"No, but I do." His playful smile deepened into a serious line. "You're good for me, Cassie. You make me want to be better." He touched his forehead to mine. "I hope someday I can make you feel the same way. That I can be good for you."

"You are good for me." I cupped his handsome face and nuzzled our mouths together. "You're good *to* me."

"I like being good to you." His eyes turned dark as he growled, "But I like doing bad things with you." He nipped at my lower lip. "Dirty things that make you blush." He kissed my neck, and I shuddered. "Filthy things that make you so wet I feel like I might drown when I bury my face between your thighs."

"Hagen," I whispered, scandalized.

"Let's take a shower." His deep voice tumbled through me.

"Then we'll see what else I can do to make you blush that pretty again."

I smiled as he drained the last of his beer and stepped over to the sink to rinse it before dropping it in the recycling container I had convinced him to use. He didn't share my enthusiasm for eco-friendly living, but he had agreed to small changes here and there. I appreciated his willingness to try.

I hopped off the counter and held out my hand, silently beckoning him to follow me. He grasped my hand and followed closely as we made our way upstairs, turning off lights and tugging me toward the front door to check the security system. By the time we reached his bedroom, we were both grinning and breathing hard from stolen kisses as we raced upstairs.

I toed off my sneakers in the bedroom and removed my earrings and watch before I joined Hagen in his lavish bathroom. His entire house was beautifully modern with a calming palette of white and grey and black. The bathroom was no different with dove grey flooring, dark grey concrete countertops and blond wood accents. The oversized shower was tiled in grey and black with mosaic flooring.

Hagen emerged from the walk-in closet barefoot and without his watch or cuff links. He reached into the shower to turn on the water and I crossed the floor to join him. I plucked through the buttons on his shirt, pausing just long enough to let him drag the black hair tie from my wrist. I was too short to push the shirt from his shoulders so he shrugged out of it and peeled away his undershirt, throwing it aside.

When I started to unbuckle his belt, he combed his fingers through my hair, gathering it high into the loose bun he had learned I liked to wear in the shower. His big hands were always so gentle when he touched me. Sometimes, I would think back to our first encounter in that back room of his bar. I had been terrified of him. He was this hulking, arrogant loan shark who had my brother's life in his hands. I had been afraid he would hurt me to get my brother to settle his debts, but he had offered me a trade—my body for the debt.

At first, I had been furious that he would offer something so degrading, but later, when I understood him better, I had realized he was afraid of me, afraid of what I thought of him, afraid that I would run and never look back. For all his infamy in the Houston underworld, he was reserved and quiet and preferred to blend into the background. He wasn't flashy. He wasn't loud. He was steadfast, deliberate. He never did anything without calculating the risks and outcomes.

I loved him for it. After losing my parents in a horrible car accident and almost losing my brother to his gambling addiction, I craved stability. I needed a partner I could trust to follow through on his promises. I needed a partner who understood the importance of my studies and what I wanted to do with my life. I had found that partner in the most unlikely way.

"Get this off," he urged, his voice husky and low as he tugged on my shirt. Without waiting for me to do it, he grabbed the bottom of it and dragged it up and over my head. My bra hardly slowed him, and he quickly flicked through the hooks. I pushed down his slacks and boxer-briefs together, not at all surprised to see his stiff erection waiting for me. With a sheepish grin, he said, "Sorry."

He swooped down and kissed me before I could answer.

His hands were more insistent, rougher, as they tugged on my jeans and panties. He lifted me up, and I kicked them the rest of the way off before wrapping my legs around his waist. He moved effortlessly, carrying me into the spacious shower and right under the multiple sprays of soothing hot water. We kissed lazily, neither of us ready to let go just yet. I didn't think I would ever get tired of being held by him, of having his powerful arms around me or his tender mouth on mine.

When he finally let me slide down to my feet, he stepped back under the nearest shower head. He scrubbed his fingers through his dark hair and reached for the bottle of shampoo on the high shelf. I enjoyed the sight of his muscled body moving, his strong hands and chiseled arms flexing as he worked his hair into a lather. The heat of the shower amplified the tea tree and lemon scents, and I breathed it in, happy to be so close to him again.

After he rinsed his hair, he grabbed his bar of soap and stalked toward me. His playful grin sent a frisson if excitement through me. The rich lather he worked between his hands felt like liquid silk against my skin as he swept his palms over my body. He seemed to always enjoy drawing out foreplay, to leave me aching and desperate for his touch. Tonight was no different.

"I couldn't stop thinking about you," he confessed as his soapy fingers swept along my inner thigh. "I fucked my hand every night thinking of you."

"Like this?" I grasped the hard length of him and stroked slowly.

He let loose a sound that was half laugh, half growl. "Just like that."

His mouth teased across mine as I slid my hand up and down his shaft. I nipped at his bottom lip as I stroked him the way he liked best. His hands moved over my body, spreading suds and the wicked heat of anticipation.

"I have got to get a bench in here," he groaned. "This height difference is killing us."

"Sorry," I murmured against his jaw. "I should have eaten more vegetables as a kid."

He laughed and kissed me again before maneuvering me under the nearest shower head. When we were rinsed, he shut off the water and stepped out to grab a towel for me. Desperate to continue what we had started, I hurriedly toweled off and all but skipped into the bedroom. I climbed onto the bed, still warm from the shower, and waited for him.

He stalked toward me, and I rose up on my knees, reaching out for him. When I finally had my hands on his incredible body, I knew exactly what I wanted. Clutching his hips, I leaned forward and grazed my lips along the length of his cock. Looking up at him, I held his gaze as I moved my open mouth over the tip and sucked.

"Cassie," he whispered. Shuddering, he groaned and thrust carefully. Like the rest of him, his cock was huge, and I still hadn't mastered the ability to take all of him like this. He swore he didn't care, but I couldn't shake the worry that I wasn't skilled enough.

His hands moved toward my hair, gently untangling the hair tie and combing his fingers through my slightly damp hair. He gathered my hair in his fist at the base of my head and tilted my head back just slightly. His nostrils flared as he pushed a little deeper. I held his dark gaze as he worked his cock in and out of my willing mouth.

Hands on his thighs, I balanced myself and let him take control. He wouldn't hurt me. He wouldn't take advantage of my trust or try to force me to give him more. It was hard to explain, but the knowledge that I was safe in his hands, even in a situation like this, made me crave him even more.

"That's enough," he growled, dragging his cock free. His thumb wiped my lips before pushing between them. I sucked on it, drawing a deep groan from him. Bending down, he captured my mouth in a punishing kiss and grasped the backs of my thighs. In a smooth move, he lifted me off the bed and guided my legs around his waist. He was ruthless with his kisses, and I clung to him, arms around his shoulders as he left me breathless.

Without warning, he turned and dropped back onto the bed. I gasped at the sudden fall and then giggled against his neck. Draped on top of him, I straddled his hips and enjoyed being eye to eye with him for once. His gruff, rumbling laughter faded away as I dotted soft kisses along his jaw. The stubble on his skin was sure to leave me red but I didn't care.

"I missed you so much," I murmured against his jaw. Emboldened by the heat reflected in his eyes, I admitted," You're not the only one who had to take matters into their own hands."

Hagen's hands tightened on my waist. "Poor baby," he said, his hand sliding down to cup my bottom. "Left alone and neglected." His other hand moved to the back of my upper thigh. "Get up here and let me apologize."

"Hagen!" I cried out in shock as he hauled me up his body. He didn't stop until my knees were on either side of his head.

Scandalized by the idea of sitting on his face, I tried to wiggle away. "I can't."

"Stop." He nipped my inner thigh. "Relax."

"That's easy for you to say," I grumbled, embarrassed and unable to meet his gaze.

"Of course it is," he replied before nibbling on my other thigh. "I'm about to put my tongue in my favorite place."

Knowing he wouldn't be swayed and desperately wanting to feel his mouth on me, I closed my eyes and slid down onto him. He groaned happily and held tight to my thighs, pulling me forward and right onto his mouth. At the first touch of his tongue, all of my insecurities and inhibitions fled.

I dropped forward, palms against the mattress, and widened my thighs, tucking my calves under his shoulders to anchor myself. His enthusiastic licking did crazy things to me. My toes curled and I clawed at the bed as his tongue swirled and flicked, pushing me closer and closer to the edge.

When one and then two of his thick fingers slipped into my slick heat, I gasped. I sat up straighter, every muscle taut as his mouth and hand did wicked things to me. Unable to help myself, I swiveled my hips against him, drawing out the pressure and pleasure. Staring down at him, seeing his face between thighs, sent me careening off the ledge.

"Hagen!" Coming so hard I saw stars, I surrendered to the wild feelings his mouth evoked. He gripped my thighs so tightly, holding me in place while his tongue lashed me, that I knew I would have fingertip bruises in the morning. The very thought of being marked by him only made me moan louder.

When it was over, I slumped forward, panting and shuddering as he licked and suckled me through the aftershocks of pleasure. He kissed my thighs and rubbed my lower back, easing me down in that loving way of his. Limp from my orgasm, I fell onto my side, reaching for him and silently begging him to fuck me.

Hagen followed my wordless plea, pushing up onto his knees and grabbing me by the waist. He hauled me in front of him, canting my hips up and pushing my thighs apart so he could slot himself into me. My forehead dropped down to the bed, and I pushed back toward him, wanting him inside me. "Please."

"You want my cock?" He teased me with it, dragging it down the wetness and rubbing the head of it against my extremely sensitive clit. "Take it," he ordered. "Take my dick and show me where you want it."

Breathing hard, I reached back between my legs and grasped the hard length of him. I could feel the heated pulse as I guided him into me, pushing back against his huge cock until it was inside me. "Here. I want you here."

He groaned and gripped my waist, taking control. He was agonizingly gentle. His thrusts were slow and shallow. He eased his way deeper into me, his shaft gliding in my wetness until he was buried as far as he could go. There was a moment of delicious discomfort, the heady mix of pleasure heightened by that hint of pain. When he retreated, the slide of his cock made me shiver, and I clutched at the duvet, fisting it tightly as he started to move.

His rhythm increased, and I rocked on my knees, taking all he had to give. Hagen kept one hand on my waist and the other grabbed a handful of my hair, drawing my chin up and my back straight. The angle of his thrusting felt incredible, and the endless moans escaping my throat told him exactly that. I wasn't close to another orgasm, but it didn't matter. I enjoyed making him feel good more than chasing another climax.

He shifted behind me and planted his foot next to my elbow. He let go of my hair and took hold of my shoulder. The force of his thrusts increased, and I reached out to grab his foot, desperate for something to hold onto as he fucked me like a wild man.

But his next stroke went too far. Too deep. Too hard. Too fast. I gasped, shocked at the bright surge of pain, and he instantly stopped. Carefully, he withdrew and turned me over, his huge hands cradling my hip and my upper back. He gazed down at me with such concern that it made my heart ache. "Are you okay?"

"I'm fine."

"You didn't sound fine," he insisted, his voice laced with worry. "I have to be more careful with you."

"Hagen," I whispered and stroked his jaw, "you are always careful with me. Weird things happen during sex. You stopped without having to be asked. That's all that matters."

"I'm sorry," he apologized again, even though he didn't need to say the words.

"There's nothing to forgive," I murmured and slowly wrapped my legs around his waist. With my heels against his ass, I drew him forward. "Come back to me."

He swallowed hard. "You sure?"

I reached between our bodies and grasped the stiff length of him. Holding his gaze, I pressed him into my slick heat. "I'm sure."

"Fuck," he growled and rocked into me. "This okay?"

"Yes," I said, head thrown back as I felt his body rubbing mine in all the right ways. I clung to his shoulders as he made love to me, his pace steady and true. "Hagen."

He buried his face against me, nipping and kissing my neck before claiming my mouth. When his hand slid down to cup my bottom, lifting it higher and giving him the perfect angle, I cried out in pleasure. He smiled triumphantly and used his considerable strength to manhandle me right where he wanted me. "Rub your clit, Cassie. I want to feel you squeeze me when I come."

His filthy instruction sent a ripple of white-hot excitement right through me. I slid my hand down my belly to where our bodies were joined. I was so wet, making an absolute mess of both of us, and my fingertips slid easily over my sensitive clitoris. It didn't take much to get there. A few insistent, steady circles, and I shattered, keening loudly and rearing up into him, my thighs tightening around his waist as he thrust into me over and over until he groaned and shuddered.

"Fuck, I love you." His declaration came out on a panted breath. He kissed me then, his mouth languid and soft as he pulsed inside me. He pulled back a few inches and brushed the damp hair from my face. "I love you, Cassie."

"I love you, John." I didn't use his first name often, keeping it for those special or important moments between us. He smiled tenderly and kissed me one last time before withdrawing and dramatically falling onto the bed next to me. Wordlessly, he dragged me closer and kept me in his arms as we enjoyed the warm, hazy afterglow.

I wasn't sure which one of us fell asleep first. When I came to later, I glanced at the bedside clock and saw that it was after midnight. Grimacing at the wet mess between my thighs, I carefully disentangled myself from his arms and practically ran to the bathroom. After I tidied up, I picked up the trail of clothing that started by the doorway and ended in the bathroom. I pulled our phones from the pockets of our pants and carried them back to the bedroom when I was done throwing our clothes in the hamper and hanging our towels on their hooks.

My phone was almost dead, and his battery indicator was yellow. I carried them to the charging station on his side of the bed and plugged the annoying little cords into place. I scrolled down my phone's screen to see if I had missed anything important. The Instagram posts on Taylor's private account were amusing, and I had a feeling she would be sleeping off one hell of a hangover tomorrow.

As I put my phone down next to Hagen's, his screen lit up with a message. I wasn't trying to snoop, not really, but the name on the message—Amber—caught my eye. Her number's area code was familiar. I had been doing so much research on California, especially CalTech and Stanford, to recognize a San Francisco area code when I saw one.

My heart pounded in my throat as I read the flirty message. I had to reread it four times to be sure I wasn't misunderstanding it.

Amber: Even if you decide not to let my firm handle your money, I'd love to have a chance to handle you. I'm available for a more in-depth demonstration of our hands-on style of managing our clients.

Overcome with the fear, I glanced at Hagen's sleeping

form. What, exactly, had happened during his trip? He had seemed so open and honest during our conversation over dinner that I couldn't believe he had been lying or holding back details.

I put his phone down and climbed back into bed. My stomach was a mess of knots as my insecurities took hold. The what-ifs tormented me, and I started to doubt myself and everything I believed to be true.

Hagen's big hand settled onto my hip, and he dragged me across the space between us, pulling my back against his chest. He nuzzled into my neck and draped his arm across my waist. His sleepy kisses soothed my fears. Hagen wouldn't cheat on me. He wasn't that kind of man.

Was he?

CHAPTER THREE

"**M**Y HEAD IS killing me," Taylor whined pitifully.

"Well, stop harassing me on the phone, and go to bed early," I suggested while throwing my wet clothes into the dryer. "Or call that paramedic you used to date and see if he has any bags of saline squirreled away in his apartment."

"Oh, that's a good idea," Taylor replied, her voice lifting hopefully. "I bet he could hook me up with some hydration therapy." She paused. "Ugh. But he'll probably want me to blow him or something gross like that."

I snorted and dropped quarters into the slots for the dryer. "That's quite a quandary you face."

She sighed. "Fuck it. I'm calling him."

"Be safe," I urged.

"Always!"

Shaking my head at her antics, I tucked my phone into the thigh pocket of my leggings and put my other load of laundry into the washer. There were four other sets of washers and dryers in the community laundry room, but I tried to only use one set, even if I had more than one load and it meant double the time. With all the single moms and families in the complex, I had more flexibility on doing my laundry and didn't want to be that selfish ass keeping a tired mom from getting her chores finished.

As I left the laundry room to check my mail, I could hear Hagen's voice in my head, telling me to use his washer and dryer. If he had his way, I would have moved in with him by now. He didn't see the point in me paying rent when he had a perfectly good house where I was always welcome.

There were so many times when I wanted to cave and accept his offer. The thought of having more than seven hundred square feet of space and access to a nicer kitchen with actual pantry storage was tempting. Too tempting.

He liked to take care of me and wanted to give me an easier life. I liked standing on my own two feet and supporting myself. It was the only disagreement in our relationship, and I worried it would cause strain as things grew even more serious between us. Hagen was older than me and ready for that next stage of life—a shared house, kids, HOA meetings and retirement plans. I was just getting started and on the cusp of making a huge decision about my future. In a few months, I would be choosing a grad school and moving far away from Houston.

And away from Hagen.

The thought of leaving him made my heart ache and my stomach clench painfully. I had considered staying at Rice or looking at other in-state options, but the very best graduate programs were in California or Massachusetts. I had the education, the grades and the GRE scores to get into the very best universities. I couldn't give up the chance to realize my dreams of working in astronautics and space engineering to stay close to Hagen.

Not that he would ever ask me to do that. I believed him

when he told me how proud he was of me or how excited he was for my future. I believed that he wanted the absolute best for me. I wanted the best for him. I wanted him to have an equally as promising future.

But how the hell did we meld our two lives together to make sure we were both happy? I couldn't imagine asking him to sell his home, his businesses, sever his ties and pack up to move with me. He had established himself here, and he had earned his place in the business community. He deserved to stay here where his future was the most predictable and steady.

Troubled by those thoughts, I jammed my mailbox key into the rusty slot and fought with the door until it creaked open and dropped with a clang. Like everything else at the complex, the mail station needed some serious maintenance. For the rent I paid, I couldn't complain even if I was bothered and frustrated by the ongoing problems—like the cracked sidewalk I stumbled over as I flicked through my mail on my walk back to the laundry room.

A sealed envelope from the apartment complex caught my eye. I had a bad feeling as I stared at it. They never sent out mailed notices. Whatever it was must have been important and probably bad news. Not wanting to deal with it, I tucked it into the middle of the pile of mail.

When I walked into the laundry room, I noticed the last two people I wanted to see. My footsteps faltered, and I honestly considered turning and running before they spotted me. Janine and her boyfriend Travis had no love for me. I didn't blame them. Travis had been Ronnie's weed dealer and had later introduced him to the local underground gambling scene. When Ronnie had left Houston on Hagen's dime, he had left behind a few unsettled debts. The biggest ones Hagen had graciously settled, sparing my brother from certain death, but the smaller ones, the ones to men like Travis and the dice and card game hosts he hung out with had gone unpaid.

From the nasty looks I got from Travis and the angry vitriol Janine often spewed at me, I knew they had both suffered because of the unpaid debts. I had wanted to pay them, but Hagen forbid it. His reasons made sense—that I would be opening myself up to more debt claims or that I could end up paying an undercover cop and put my future at risk—but they didn't make it any easier to bear Janine and Travis's ire.

Steeling myself for the inevitable nastiness, I strode toward the washer and dryer I had been using. I noticed Janine's smug smirk, and my stomach dropped. A few more steps, and I saw why she was so pleased with herself. My half-washed clothing was in the trashcan. I could only assume that my laundry from the dryer was in the same place.

Refusing to let them know they had upset me, I calmly bent down to grab my laundry baskets she had thrown into the corner. At the last second, I stopped and managed to not touch the absolutely disgusting droplets of urine on the plastic. Someone—Travis, probably—had pissed all over my laundry baskets. Appalled, I glanced back at Janine and she shot me the finger before mouthing, "Fuck you."

"Hey, let me help," Kyle said, startling me as he appeared suddenly behind me. He had his own small basket of laundry on his hip, and I smile gratefully at him. When he noticed the urine puddles in my baskets, he wrinkled his nose and snarled, "Those fucking assholes."

"What did you say?" Travis asked from across the laundry

room.

Kyle straightened up and turned toward him. "You two are lowlife fucking scum."

"Real tough words from you, soy boy," Travis snapped.

Kyle rolled his eyes. "Soy boy? Yeah. That's real fucking original. You read that in your 4Chan circle jerk?"

"You prefer cuck?" Travis glanced at me before adding, "Everyone sees the way you keep chasing her around, but she's only got eyes for that big-dicked loan shark."

"You are so gross," I said, disgusted with him. Touching Kyle's arm, I pleaded, "Let's just get out of here."

Kyle's eyes were narrowed with anger, but he nodded and helped me gather up my wet clothing. I didn't waste time picking off the trash and lint sticking to my soggy laundry. I grabbed one armful, and Kyle took another, dropping it on top of his basket. We left my baskets there, neither of us wanting to touch them. He followed me out of the laundry room, down the sidewalk to the building where we both lived.

"You need to report them to the management," Kyle urged.

"So they can retaliate even more?"

"Call the police then," he said.

"And say what? That my brother ran out on some drug and gambling debts and I'm being harassed because I won't pay them?" I shook my head. "That's more trouble than I need."

"Is it a lot?" Kyle adjusted his grip on the heavy basket. "What Ronnie owes?"

"I don't know," I admitted. "I don't *want* to know."

"Why can't you ask Hagen for the money?"

"He's not an ATM," I replied with a frown. "And, anyway, he's already done so much to help my brother. I'm not going to ask him to open his wallet again."

"You shouldn't have to ask. He should volunteer to help you, if he loves you."

"He *does* love me. It's not his job to ride in like my knight in shining armor and save me every time I have problems."

"Yes, it is," Kyle insisted. "That's the whole point of a relationship. The man is supposed to take care of his woman. Doesn't he want you to be safe?"

"Of course, he does," I replied, more harshly than intended. "He would do anything for me."

"Except pay these debts?"

"Pay what debts?" Hagen's voice startled both of us. He had been leaning against my door, waiting for me. He pushed off of it and removed his aviators. His gaze moved from my face to the wet clothing, and his jaw clenched. "What happened?"

"Just a little disagreement in the laundry room," I said airily, not wanting him to go full-blown knee breaking loan shark on Janine and Travis.

"They took her clothes out of the machines, threw them in the trash and used the money in the machines to wash their own laundry," Kyle said, ratting me out to Hagen. "They also pissed on her laundry baskets."

Hagen's nostrils flared. "Stay here."

"Hagen," I pleaded, "don't."

He ignored my plea and stormed down the sidewalk, his long strides purposeful and strong. In his jeans and grey Henley with those black boots, he looked tough and mean. I wanted to chase after him, to tell him not to make trouble, but I stayed put. Some part of me, a part of me I hated to acknowledge, liked his alpha protectiveness.

"We should probably get inside," Kyle suggested, his arms straining under the weight of the wet laundry stacked on top of his.

"Right," I said, tearing my gaze away from Hagen's back. Arms full of wet clothing, I realized I couldn't reach my keys. "Can you grab my keyring out of my pocket? It's on this side."

"Sure." Kyle braced the heavy basket of clothes against the wall and plucked the keys from the thigh pocket on my leggings. I ignored the touch of his fingers a little too high on my thigh, certain it had been an accident as he tried to hold up the basket and find the keys. "Got 'em."

I stepped to the side so he could unlock my door. He followed me inside to the kitchen where we dumped my wet clothes in the, thankfully, empty sink. He pulled my mail from the back of his jeans where he had tucked it earlier and handed it over to me. "Looks like you got a rent increase, too."

"Is it bad?" My budget was tight, and I wasn't even sure where I would start to make cuts if I had to pay higher rent.

"Twenty percent."

"Shit."

"It's only a problem for you if you're staying to do your graduate work here," he reasoned. "Your lease is June to June, right?"

"No, it's month to month. Before Ronnie left, I had been thinking about switching complexes to a place closer to the university. They only had two-bedroom units available which was perfect because he could share the rent with me, but then he had to leave and I missed my lease re-up deadline."

"And they put you on month-to-month," he finished for me.

"Yeah."

"Well. Shit. That sucks." With a shrug, Kyle said, "Listen, if push comes to shove and you can't afford it, I've got an empty bedroom right across the hall."

"I can't push you out of your office." It was the easiest way to turn down his offer without looking rude. Even though we were friends, I wouldn't be comfortable sharing a living space with him. Not to mention, Hagen would lose his shit if I moved in with another man.

"I can shift it. No problem," he added with a smile. "Anything I can do to help, I will."

Not for the first time, I suspected Kyle had more than just friendly feelings for me. I hadn't done anything to encourage him to think we would ever be anything more than friends, and I was open about how much I loved Hagen and how happy he made me. Even so, it seemed as if Kyle may have been harboring hopes.

Before I could try to make things clear, Hagen returned, his footsteps heavy as he walked toward the kitchen. His gaze darted from Kyle to me, lingering on the short distance between us, and his eyes narrowed briefly. I rolled my eyes at his obvious flare of jealousy.

"Think about it," Kyle said before patting my shoulder and leaving my apartment.

After the door closed, Hagen asked, "Think about what?"

"Moving in with him."

"Like fucking hell," Hagen growled. "If you're moving anywhere, it's in with me. Which I've been asking you to do for weeks," he reminded me with a pointed look. "Why would you need to move in with Kyle anyway?"

"Apparently, my rent is going up," I said, reaching for my mail. As I opened the envelope, I asked, "Did you punch Travis?"

He frowned down at me. "No."

"Did you threaten him?"

"A little," he admitted, moving closer to me. His big hand cupped my face, and he brushed his thumb over my cheek. "He's buying new laundry baskets, and he's not going to bother you anymore about Ronnie's bullshit."

"Please tell me you did not just pay more of my brother's debts. You have already done too much."

"I didn't pay that lowlife anything. After all the work I've done to keep my earnings and my business clean, I'm not about to risk it by handing money over to someone like that meth head. I have a pretty good idea where he gets his product and where he was taking Ronnie to gamble. I'm not putting my money anywhere near that."

"Good." Glad that he hadn't extended himself even more for my brother, I pulled the notice out of the envelope and scanned it. I grimaced at the new amount due on the first of the next month. "Shit."

Hagen moved behind me so he could read the letter. "You are not paying that much for this place."

"I don't have that much to pay for it," I admitted, feeling embarrassed by just how tight my budget was these days. With all the fees for my GRE prep courses, the exam, the fees for submitting applications to different schools—I was tapped out.

"Cassie," Hagen said tenderly, his hands settling on my waist as he bent down to nuzzle my neck, "move in with me. This place is a nightmare, and you have so much stress in your life. Let me take some of that stress away for you. Come live with me. Save your money for grad school."

For weeks, I had been fighting against my desire to be closer to him, to share his living space and merge our lives. It came from a place of pride and fear. There was always the what-if in the back of my mind. What if we realized we weren't compatible? What if our hopes and dreams for the future didn't mesh? What if he stopped loving me? Where would I go then? A hotel? My car? A friend's couch?

Turning in his arms, I gazed up at him and all of those worries fled. "Okay."

He grinned. "Yeah?"

"Yeah." I rose on tiptoes, signaling I wanted a kiss, and he happily met me more than halfway.

Like a little kid on Christmas morning, he vibrated with excitement. "Let's get you packed."

"Right now?" I laughed. "We don't have any boxes."

"Right," he said, abashed. "Pack a suitcase. We'll take your laundry with us. We can figure out the logistics of your move later."

"Sounds good," I agreed, filled with a sudden rush of relief and happiness. After another kiss, both of us smiling like fools, I hurried to my bedroom closet and grabbed my suitcase. It didn't take long to pack for a few days. When I came back to the kitchen, Hagen stood over my sink, wringing out my wet clothing. The muscles in his arms rippled with his twisting movements, and I was struck by how incredibly powerful he was. It wasn't hard to imagine how easily he could use those hands of his to hurt someone. Yet, when his hands were on me, they were always gentle and loving.

"You enjoying your front row seat to the gun show?" he asked with a playful smirk.

I snorted and rolled my eyes. "I've seen better."

"Uh-huh," he said, wringing out the last pair of jeans. "Not from that pencil-dicked creep across the hall."

"He's not a creep," I admonished. "He's a good guy."

Hagen grunted and pulled a trash bag from the box under the sink. "A good guy who is waiting for me to stumble so he can swoop in and steal you."

"Like Amber?" I asked, letting the accusatory question slip out before I could stop it.

Frowning, Hagen stopped stuffing my wet clothes into the trash bag and leveled a strange look my way. "I don't think she's strong enough to pick me up and steal me."

"Be serious, John."

He set aside the bag and closed the distance between us. He put his hands on my shoulders and gazed down at me, his stare unwavering as he said, "I'm serious about you. I'm serious about us. I assume you saw that text message she sent last night."

He wasn't asking but I nodded. "I was plugging in our phones to charge when it popped up on the screen."

"I told her not to contact me again. She was way out of line using my contact info to proposition me." His hands moved from my shoulders to my neck and up to cup my face. "Cassie, you're the only one I want."

Closing my eyes, I stepped into him and rested my cheek

against his chest. I slid my arms around his waist and held tight. His hand stroked down the length of my ponytail and then followed the curve of my back. It felt so good to lean on him, to be held in his arms. It felt right. It felt like home.

He kissed the top of my head. "Let's get out of here, Tiny."

Smiling at his silly nickname for me, I waited for him to gather up my laundry in one hand and my suitcase in the other. I slipped into my backpack, glanced around my apartment for any necessities I might have forgotten and trailed him out to the breezeway. After I locked the door, we made our way to our vehicles.

"We should do takeout tonight," Hagen decided as I reached for my keys.

"Put the laundry in my car. I'll drive it over and get it started while you grab something for dinner."

"Sure." He accepted my suggestion with a nod. "Chinese? Thai? Pho?"

"Something spicy," I said, craving the bite and burn.

He boxed me in against my car and dipped down to brush his mouth over mine. "Drive safe. Text me when you get home."

A frisson of excitement raced through me. Home. Our home. Together.

Traffic was light, for once, and I made it to Hagen's house in record time. I pulled into the garage space he had given me and carried my laundry and suitcase inside. I separated my laundry into two loads and stuffed the first one into his gleaming front-loading washer, pressing the buttons on the dashboard that looked like something from a spaceship. Using his expensive, name brand detergent was an absolute luxury after years of buying the cheapest generic I could find.

I carried my suitcase upstairs to Hagen's room. I wasn't sure where to put my things so I decided to leave them in the suitcase for now. Later, after dinner, he could tell me which spaces were mine.

Back downstairs, I walked back into the garage and retrieved my backpack. I placed it on one of the stools in the kitchen and took out my plasma physics textbook, notebook and pouch filled with colored pens and highlighters. I opened the book to my last bookmark and neatly printed a title on the clean page of my notebook before I started reading. The upcoming lecture on electromagnetic waves in plasmas was one I had been looking forward to, and I wanted to make sure I had the reading done with enough time to work out any confusing bits before Dr. Symonds started teaching.

The sound of the side door opening interrupted my note taking. I glanced at the arched doorway between the mudroom and the kitchen and smiled at Hagen as he returned with bags crammed with takeout. Even before he reached the island where I sat, I caught the familiar and delicious scent of spicy Szechuan eggplant from our favorite Chinese restaurant. When my gaze landed on the pretty pink box from my favorite bakery—a place I only indulged every few months—I lit up with happiness.

Hagen laughed and set the box down in front of me. "I thought you agreeing to move in here was worthy of a cake."

I peeked under the lid and gasped with excitement when I saw the fluffy, rich buttercream and sprinkles. "Birthday cake!"

He laughed even harder and noisily kissed my cheek. "Don't ever change, Cass."

"Do you mind if I finish my notes while we eat?" I didn't want to be rude, but I was right in the middle of an equation.

"You don't have to stop working on whatever the hell that is," he said, gesturing to the equations I was carefully writing. "Derivation of dispersion relation?" He read my notes and shook his head. "Is that even English?"

I rolled my eyes and bumped his arm with my shoulder. "Stop. I've seen your math skills. I know you understand derivatives."

"Maybe," he replied cagily. He didn't like to admit that his book smarts matched his street smarts, especially when it came to math. It was how he had been able to make so much money. He had a keen eye for risk and probability. "But that," he pointed at my notes, "is way harder than anything I've ever done."

"You could learn," I remarked as I followed the equation to the next step. "I could teach you."

"Yeah? What are your tutoring fees?"

"For you? I could give you a deal."

"Oh?"

"Maybe we could barter something you have that I want."

"Like?" The gleam in his eyes matched mine.

"Oh," I said, drawing out the word as I walked my fingers up the denim stretched across his powerful thigh. "Maybe something like this?"

He inhaled a sharp breath as my fingers brushed across the outline of his cock. "I'm listening."

I leaned closer and cupped him, filling my hand with his hardening shaft and only too aware that my hand wasn't even close to holding all of it. I stroked him through the denim, and his breaths grew sharper and faster.

"You keep that up, and we'll be eating cold Chinese later."

His warning had the opposite effect, and I squeezed his cock. "We have a microwave."

With a growl, he snatched me right off of my stool and dragged me onto his lap. My squeal of laughter echoed off the kitchen's vaulted ceilings, but Hagen's insistent mouth silenced it. Unlike last night, when he took his time and drew out my pleasure with slow caresses, he was ravenous. He used his superior size and strength to place me onto the counter and yank off my shoes. He gripped the waistband of my leggings along with my panties and tugged them down my hips and thighs before pulling them right off my feet and throwing them aside.

Panting with excitement and anticipation, I leaned back on my palms and waited for him to pounce. He dragged a pair of fingers through my slit and grunted when he found my pussy wet for him. He held my gaze as he slipped his fingers inside me, massaging and coaxing even more wetness to flow.

With his fingers buried deep inside me, he used his free hand to unbuckle his belt and unfasten his jeans. The thick head of his cock peeked out the top of his boxer briefs, refusing to be contained a moment longer. He roughly shoved down his briefs and freed his shaft.

When he stepped closer, I wrapped my legs around his waist and welcomed him into me. The fingers that had been thrusting into me now gripped my inner thigh, marking me with my own wetness. He didn't waste time with slow and easy thrusts. Hagen slid deep, his cock stretching and pressing into me until my head fell back and I moaned.

There was nothing to do now but hold on tightly for the ride. The counter was the perfect height for him to fuck me with ease. He didn't have to worry about supporting his weight or mine. He just had to snap his hips and pound into me until we were both panting and clutching at one another.

Hagen held my gaze as he licked the pad of his thumb, slicking his skin, before he placed it over my clit. I hissed at the sharply pleasurable sensation of his finger there, and then moaned as he began to rub in tight circles. He had studied my body enough to know all its secrets, and stimulating me there was no different. He knew the exact combination to make me scream.

And scream I did.

Loud, keening wails of ecstasy as my climax descended with a crash and my tight sheath gripped and fluttered around his still thrusting cock. He didn't take long to follow me over the edge, thrusting so hard and fast that my bare bottom slid across the cold, smooth stone countertop beneath me. I shuddered beneath him, wrapping my arms around his shoulders as he leaned over me, settling his face between my breasts and his ear against my heart. It was a tender moment after something so wild.

The chime of the washer finishing its cycle interrupted our lazy kisses and whispers of love. At any other time, it would have irritated me. Now, though, it was only a small nuisance. Wasting time on laundry wasn't going to cut into the short time we had together before I had to go home or leave for class. Soon, we would have all the time in the world for little moments like these.

Hagen rucked up the front of my shirt and dotted ticklish

kisses around my navel. "Your laundry awaits, Cinderella."

"Stop!" I giggled at the sensation of his stubble raking over my sensitive belly. "You know your stubble is my weakness."

He laughed against my belly before punctuating each word he spoke with a noisy kiss. "Laundry. Dinner. Studying. Shower. Sex."

Closing my eyes and reveling in the excitement of our new arrangement, I said, "Deal."

CHAPTER FOUR

"$\mathbf{S}$O, AS WE dig deeper into this topic, you'll begin to understand how much of a profound impact these nonlinear dispersions have on the propagation of wave packets," Dr. Symonds said as she wrapped up her lecture. "I think we'll stop here today. If there are no questions?" She paused and waited for anyone in the lecture hall to raise their hand. "Okay. Feel free to email me or come by the office if you need some help."

The small class erupted into movement all around me. People started packing away their laptops and notebooks while chatting. I did the same, tucking my notebook into my well-loved backpack and hefting the straps onto my shoulders.

"Cassie? Do you have time to walk with me?" Dr. Symonds called from the front of the class.

"Yes, ma'am." I squeezed through the wall of much taller bodies blocking the stairs and worked my way down to the front of the lecture hall to meet with my mentor.

"Did you have any problems following the lecture?" Dr. Symonds asked as she picked up her worn leather messenger bag and travel mug. "You seemed to be the only face in here not frowning or looking back at me in a panic."

"I did the reading over the weekend and took some time to

work through the examples."

"Smart girl," she said with an approving smile. Gesturing toward the side entrance, she indicated we should walk. As I fell into step beside her, she said, "Have you given any more thought to your grad school picks?"

"Yes. I finalized my list yesterday."

"And?"

"CalTech, Stanford, Princeton and MIT," I listed off my top choices. Staying here at Rice was my backup plan, as she well knew.

"What was your verbal score?"

"162."

"And your quant?"

"166."

"And writing?"

"5."

She tallied up the GRE score. "333 is a strong score. With the right essays and recommendation letters, you'll get some really strong offers."

"I hope so," I said, letting worry seep into my voice. "I really want this, and it's so scary to think I might not have what it takes to make it at CalTech or Stanford."

"You have exactly what it takes," Dr. Symonds assured me. "You're smart, yes, but you're tenacious. You're a hard worker. You aren't afraid to make sacrifices. You are going to do great things someday very soon in astronautics and space engineering. Believe in yourself the way I believe in you."

Her pep talk hit me right in the feels. "I will."

"Good. Now, come see me later this week, and we'll start working on your list for recommendation letters. You also need to schedule a meeting with the grad school advising office to practice your interviews. You want to nail those. Make a great impression. Make them want you in their programs."

"I'll get right on that."

She patted my back, and we separated, her heading into her office and me toward the lab where I worked part-time. I had been extremely lucky to snag a spot in the lab as a sophomore. Dr. Symonds had recommended me, and I had started off as nothing more than a glorified gofer. After a while, I had earned my place and learned so much about black holes, magnetars and pulsars. I was able to observe laser-driven plasmas, and now helped collect, input and refine data on dark matter detection. The work I did wasn't very exciting, but it was vitally important to the research being done in this lab.

While I worked, I pushed all thoughts from my mind and concentrated on what was right in front of me. Even though I had a million things on my seemingly never-ending to-do list, my focus remained on the scads of data and the modeling I had been tasked with creating. Dark matter had always intrigued me. It was a peculiar thing, something that the scientific community had only just started to study in any depth and puzzle out with the help of computers. The implications behind dark matter—about what it was and the purpose it served—were just as mysterious as its name. I hoped that someday my work here in the lab, no matter how boring, would lead to some of the answers we all wanted.

The alarm on my watch buzzed, and I wrapped up my work, saving and closing my files and straightening my workstation. I grabbed my backpack, waved to my supervising grad student and hurried off to my afternoon class. I found my usual seat in the middle of the small classroom and checked my phone since I had a few extra minutes.

> **Hagen:** I'll be home late. Do you want me to grab dinner?
>
> **Me:** I'll cook.
>
> **Hagen:** OK.
>
> **Me:** I'm stopping by my place to do a mini purge and declutter. Cut down on the number of boxes I'll need.
>
> **Hagen:** Text me if you need help. Call me when you get home.

Seeing the professor walk in the side door, I quickly sent Hagen a thumbs-up emoji and stowed my phone in my backpack. I pulled out my notebook covered in planet stickers and found the last page I had written notes on and drew a line underneath. I printed *Radii and Temperatures* and turned my attention toward the front of the class where the professor was already scribbling hasty equations on the blackboard. He wasn't the easiest teacher to follow, but his lecture notes were all provided online. I'd had him in a previous course and knew he liked to sneak in little interesting facts and tidbits during class that would end up on his final exams. Those were things I tried to catch in my notes.

"Hey, Cass," Kunal, one of my classmates leaned forward as the lecture ended, "I hate to ask, but can I get your notes from the stat course you took last spring?"

"408?"

"Yeah." He made a face and admitted, "My course load is heavy as shit this semester, and after dad got sick—"

"Kunal," I reached out and touched his hand, "don't worry about it. You can have them. I'll bring the notebook to class on Wednesday."

"Thank you, Cass. It's just…it's been hard, you know?"

I nodded, understanding only too well how difficult it could be to adjust to the loss of a parent. His father had been their family's breadwinner, and after he died of a sudden stroke, Kunal was shouldering his late father's responsibilities to his mother and younger sisters. "If you need anything, ask. I mean it. I've been there. When my parents died, it sucked. Whatever I can do to help, I will."

"If I can think of anything else, I will." He smiled. "I'll bring you some of Mom's *pav bhaji* in exchange for the notes."

"Yes!" I grinned excitedly. His mother's food was so damn good, and the first time I'd gone to his house for dinner, I had gone home with plastic containers crammed full. "You throw in some of your mom's samosas, and I'll take your tests for you."

He laughed. "If it comes to that, I just might."

We left the classroom together, and he asked me about my GRE and my plans for grad school. "I was talking to Dr. Symonds earlier about my options. I've got a shortlist of schools. I feel pretty good about my chances. You?"

"329," he said with a pleased smile. After a moment, he added, "I took the MCAT."

"What?" I glanced at him in surprise. "I didn't know you were interested in medical school."

"I wasn't," he admitted, "but I had some time to think over the summer. My family is going to need me, and I love astronomy and astrophysics but…"

"The money," I said, understanding exactly what he meant. "We're definitely not going to get rich in this field."

"No, and I owe it to my mother and my sisters and my wife and kids someday to be able to support them well."

"Well, how did the MCAT go?"

He grinned and said, "521."

"Are you fucking serious?" I busted out in shock, stopping to gawk up at him. "521! Holy shit. Good for you, Kunal!"

"Thanks." Bashfully, he confessed, "I'm shooting for the stars on my apps. Harvard, Johns Hopkins, Stanford, Penn...," he listed off the top schools. "If I'm going to do this, I want to do it right."

"What kind of specialty do you think you'll end up in?"

"Radiology," he said with an air of certainty. "I think I'll enjoy that the most."

"I can see that. Radiation is a part of astrophysics and astronomy. The sun and all that," I reasoned.

"Exactly."

Giving him a hip bump, I drew a smile from him. "Keep me updated. I'll make you a cake when you get your acceptance letter to Harvard."

"Deal."

We split up as we reached the main entrance of the building. I hefted my backpack a little higher on my shoulders and started walking toward my car. My stomach growled, and I stopped at the Chick-fil-A closest to my apartment complex for a ginormous sweet tea and a box of their cracktastic nuggets. I munched and listened to music until I parked at my complex.

After I stopped at the office to sign the paperwork ending

my lease on the upcoming first of the month, I made my way back to my apartment. I embraced my inner Marie Kondo and started in my bedroom, picking through hangers and my dresser drawers to find the clothing that brought me joy. As the donation pile grew, I realized how long I had been holding onto things I no longer needed or wanted. There was a reason for that, something deeper I wasn't ready to acknowledge yet. Probably a side effect of losing my parents as a teenager or having to deal with Ronnie's irresponsible and dangerous behavior.

I sorted the clothing into garbage bags and wrote donation on the outside of each bag along with what it contained—tops, bottoms, dresses and skirts or miscellaneous accessories like belts and scarves. When that was done, I moved to the kitchen and started filling my canvas grocery bags with perishables from the refrigerator and freezer to take back to Hagen's place. I grabbed a few things from my pantry—oatmeal, a half-full box of cereal, some cans of soup and an unopened jar of peanut butter—and put them in another bag.

Arms loaded down with bags, I left my apartment and carried the groceries to my car. The sun had finally started to set, but the change in temperature was negligible. The suffocating, humid heat left me grimacing as I hefted the bags into the backseat of my car. On the return trip to my apartment, I decided to grab all of the remaining bags and loaded them up my arms. Straining a bit under the weight, I closed up my apartment and turned toward the parking lot.

The sun had set completely, and the night was dark, no moon glow in the sky tonight. Crickets chirped and cicadas rattled noisily in the trees. My mind was so occupied with dinner ideas that I never even saw it coming.

Something hard slammed into the right side of my head. I gasped as pain exploded along the side of my skull. My legs gave way, and I fell forward onto the uneven, broken pavement. My knees skidded across it, rending the thin fabric of my leggings, and my arms, heavy with grocery bags, hung uselessly at my side as my jaw and then cheek impacted the pavement.

I had barely managed to draw in a shocked breath when I felt another impact, this one on my upper back. I could hear something jingling as another burst of pain knocked the wind out of me. Coins, I realized in a daze. Coins in a sock that was being used to batter me like a mace.

An angry hand gripped my loosely coiled bun and jerked my head up, forcing my back to arch unnaturally. "Tell your loan shark sugar daddy that the next time he comes after my man he better make damn sure he puts me in the hospital, too. If Travis dies, I'm going to kill you. Do you understand?"

I couldn't make sense of what Janine was saying. My ears were ringing, and my head was throbbing.

Janine fisted my hair even tighter and punched me in the side of the face. She was a bigger, stronger woman, and the impact left me reeling. "Do you understand? Huh? You skinny bitch!"

"I under—under—understand," I stammered, my tongue feeling heavy in my mouth. I tasted blood and felt it running down my chin.

Janine let go of my head, and I didn't have the strength to hold it up. My chin cracked against the pavement, and I saw stars. Still angry, she kicked me twice in the side with a final kick aimed at my backside that sent me sliding across the hot, uneven pavement, scratching up my exposed skin. "You can replace your laundry baskets with this."

Pennies, nickels and dimes showered my back and head, rolling off my body and clattering onto the parking lot. The tinkling sound of the coins hitting the pavement and spinning left my head throbbing. When the last coin fell, Janine crouched down and roughly jammed the dirty sock in my mouth. "Good luck crying for help."

Then, as if she hadn't done enough, she spit in my face. "Whore."

Stunned and panting for air around the dirty sock in my mouth, I tried to free my arms from the bags. My body felt strangely detached, as if the synapses in my brain weren't firing properly. I blinked, trying to get my bearings and clear the blood from my vision. It was running down my head and pooling under me as my vision tilted and spun, taking me back to those hot summer afternoons at the playground with Ronnie. He would take hold of the merry-go-round handles and run so fast while I clutched onto the middle and imagined I was an astronaut rocketing through space.

But I wasn't in space now. I was bleeding and losing consciousness in a parking lot. The smell of oil and blood filled my nose as I finally managed to work the sock out of my mouth. Weakly, I called for help, but the lot was deserted. I had fallen between my car and another. Could anyone even see me?

Exhaustion overwhelmed me, and I started to drift, my vision turning dark and my muscles slackening. What little faculties I still possessed told me I was in bad shape. I wondered how much that sock of coins had weighed. How hard had Janine swung? What was the force of the impact? All my knowledge of physics and math was useless now. Had she cracked my skull? Was my brain bleeding?

Am I going to die?

"Cassie? Cassie!"

It was Kyle who dropped down next to me. "Oh, shit. Shit! No. No. Don't move. Stay still."

I clutched at his hand, gripping his fingers and smearing my blood on his skin. I tried to lift my head, but he urged me to be still as he held his phone to his ear. Vaguely, I was aware of him talking to a 9-1-1 dispatcher. I squeezed his hand, my strength failing, and said, "John. Call John."

"I will, Cassie," Kyle promised, his phone clamped between his ear and his shoulder. "Just don't move, okay? There's an ambulance coming."

"Ronnie," I murmured, feeling exhaustion take hold. Someone had to call my brother.

"No. Cassie! Stay awake!" He touched my face, his fingers sliding in the blood. "No. She's passing out. Are they close? Jesus. I think she's dying."

Maybe I was.

CHAPTER FIVE

"Cassie? Cassie? Can you open your eyes?" A booming male voice drew me out of the lethargic darkness. "Hey! There you are!"

Unable to focus, I saw two of the same face above me. His dark eyes were kind but concerned as he flashed a pen light in my face. "I'm Shawn. I'm a nurse here in the ER. You're at Memorial Hermann. Can you tell me your name?"

"Cassandra," I croaked. "Cassie."

"Last name?"

My brain knew the answer, but my mouth wouldn't make the sounds. I felt as if I were drowning in quicksand, my whole body sinking into the depths of something heavy and suffocating.

"Do you know what date it is?"

"Tuesday," I answered, my thoughts all muddled. My tongue felt wrong in my mouth, and I slurred as I spoke. "No. No. It's Monday. Plasma physics. Monday. Wednesday. Friday."

"Who is the president?"

"Apprentice," I murmured, feeling sleepy again. A stab of pain on my left arm jolted me awake momentarily. Blearily, I lifted my head, my sore neck protesting the movement, and saw another nurse working a large needle into a vein.

At my whimper of pain, Shawn touched my shoulder. "Your IV blew. We're putting in a new one. We need to be able to give you fluids and medicine."

I didn't even try to protest as they cut away my clothes and moved my body for x-rays and to catalog my injuries.

"Okay. What's happening with our patient?" A commanding female voice filtered across the din of beeping machines and nurses talking. "GCS?"

"Nine when EMS picked her up but she's trending down…"

I closed my eyes as Shawn spoke to the doctor and gave her a rundown of my condition. I didn't fight against the uncomfortable testing that followed as the doctor poked at my feet and prodded other places. My head spun as she barked out orders for more tests and asked for an operating room to be reserved, just in case.

"Cassie, I'm Dr. Choi." A beautiful older woman appeared over me and gave me a reassuring smile. I blinked rapidly as I tried to focus on the double images of her. Which one was her? Which one was the extra? "I'm a neurosurgeon, and I'll be taking care of you tonight. You took some bad hits. Your boyfriend told the paramedics it was coins?"

"In a sock," I managed to say. "Hagen is here?"

"Kyle," another nurse interjected. "He's in the waiting room."

"Not my boyfriend," I said. "Hagen is."

"Cassie," Dr. Choi checked my pupils, "I am very concerned about what's going on in your brain." She frowned and started to palpate my head. "Your skull feels intact, but I'm worried you may have bleeding underneath it. We're going to do some more tests, but it's possible I may need to operate to relieve pressure if there is bleeding."

I couldn't hold back the tears or my pathetically weak sob.

"Hey, it's okay," Dr. Choi said as she gently squeezed my hand. "You're in good hands here."

Shawn took control as the doctor left, and before I knew it, I was rolling out of the ER and down a hall to the CT room. It was a quick test, and I was back in the ER, waiting my fate a short time later. The nurses and techs who streamed in and out of my room were so kind. They soothed my panic with their sure hands and warm smiles. My fuzzy thoughts seemed to clear as the minutes ticked by, and I managed to convince myself that I wasn't going to die after all.

"Cassie?" Dr. Choi returned to my bedside. "I've had a look at your CT."

"And?" I asked, terrified to hear her answer.

"You have a small epidural hematoma. We can treat it conservatively. I can have you admitted and kept under observation."

"But?"

"But there's a risk to waiting," she explained carefully. "It takes time to get a patient who is crashing down to the operating room. When you're talking about the brain, those seconds are precious. I think you would benefit from having the bleeding removed now while it's small."

"How?" My voice sounded so small and childlike as I imagined the horror that awaited me.

"It will be a very short and simple procedure. I'll make a tiny incision on your scalp. I'll drill a small hole into your skull. We'll suction out the blood to relieve the pressure on your brain. I'll place a drainage tube that will stay in place until the bleeding is resolved. You'll be in the operating room for less than an hour. If everything goes well, you'll be home and resting in a week."

Visions of drills and blood made my stomach churn. I wanted to run away. I wanted to escape. I didn't want anyone poking around in my brain.

But...

"I'm a scientist," I said, crying now. My head throbbed as I wept, but I had to get it out. My words were slow and some of them slurred as I tried to explain the situation. "All my life I've wanted to work in space. It's all I know. It's all I want. I have to be able to think. To do math. To do physics. So, whatever it takes to fix my brain? You do it."

"I'll take good care of you, Cassie," Dr. Choi promised.

There was a sudden rush of activity as the nurses and techs prepared me for surgery. I asked about Hagen, but Shawn shook his head. "Your friend hasn't been able to reach him."

"My brother?"

"I'm not sure. I'll check."

Feeling so alone, I tried not to cry, but I was so scared. My stomach lurched suddenly, and before I could warn anyone, I vomited uncontrollably. Thankfully, Shawn was ready with the pink basin that had been sitting on my bed since I arrived in the emergency room. He and another nurse quickly rotated me onto my side, preventing me from choking or aspirating. "It's okay," he said gently. "Get it out. It's the head injury."

I groaned and tried to touch my pounding head. My arms felt so heavy, and I dropped them. "Sorry."

"It's okay. We're used to it." Shawn wiped my face and made the basin disappear. "Let me see those pretty eyes, Cassie."

I blinked as he shined the pen light at me, checking my pupils. My vision seemed even blurrier now, and I was seeing four of everything. All four of Shawn's jaws flexed, and I knew it wasn't good as he said more medical things I didn't understand. The nurses and techs stepped up their speed, and in no time, I was being rolled down a hallway and into an elevator. I closed my eyes as the world started to spin again. The beep of the machine tracking my heartbeat started to speed up, and I wondered if I was about to have a heart attack on top of everything else.

When we neared the operating room, Shawn and the other nurse and tech stepped away from me as others came into view. Shawn smiled down at me and patted my hand. "You're in good hands, Cassie."

"Thank you," I managed weakly.

New nurses and techs took over, all of them in scrubs and their faces covered. I was transferred to the operating table and an anesthesiologist talked to me about the upcoming procedure and what to expect. The idea of being awake while a surgeon drilled into my skull sent my heart rate skyrocketing, and the anesthesiologist gave me something that left me feeling calm and detached.

Someone—a nurse or doctor—started asking me questions and giving me words and numbers to remember. I couldn't read the cards held up in front of me, and I started to worry that I was going to end up blind. The cold room was brightly lit, so bright it made my eyes hurt, and I closed them as the nurses and techs moved by body into the correct position. My head was secured, but there was no sensation of claustrophobia when I realized I couldn't move.

Whatever the anesthesiologist was pumping into my veins was working. I didn't even question the nurse who began to clip away a small area of my hair or flinch when they started sticking needles of anesthetic into my scalp to numb it.

"Cassie? It's time, okay?" Dr. Choi stood in front of me, her face covered with a mask and shield. The lighting had been dimmed in the background. The surgical lamps above me were bright white. I could hear nurses shuffling around behind me, moving equipment and supplies.

Unable to nod, I said, "Okay."

Dr. Choi moved out of my field of vision, stepping behind the drapes around my head. The anesthesiologist touched my hand, and said, "Just a little something to make you sleepy."

My body relaxed, and I fixed my gaze on the wall across from me. Whether it was the drugs or the exhaustion or the brain bleed itself, I felt like a balloon floating above my own body. I could hear Dr. Choi talking to her assistant and the nurses. She spoke steadily, her voice clear and calm as she worked. When the drill started to whir, I tried to go somewhere else in my mind.

Hagen.

He was my safe place.

Or he was.

Janine's angry words came roaring back to me. She had attacked me because Hagen had hurt Travis. Badly, if she was to be believed.

My emotions were muted by the medications, but I could

still feel the burn of betrayal and the heartbreak of disappointment. Later, when the medications wore off, I wouldn't be able to handle the emotional pain. I wasn't strong in that way. I had been damaged by the death of my parents, and my reaction to Hagen putting me in so much danger would be one so brutally painful it might kill me.

"Cassie, we're done."

As if the invisible balloon I had been tethered to was losing helium, I felt myself float back into my body. My head still throbbed, but it was a different sort of pain, blunt and not sharp. Groggy but relieved, I let go.

CHAPTER SIX

T HE SENSATION OF something squeezing my arm woke me. Blinking with confusion, I glanced around the hospital room. The memories came rushing back, and I closed my eyes again. The band squeezing my arm suddenly loosened. *Blood pressure cuff*, I thought at the soft hiss of air.

"Cassie?" Hagen's familiar voice drew my attention away from the band squeezing my left arm to the right side of my bed. My vision crossed, and I blinked a few more times to clear it. When that didn't work, I tried to focus on just one of the images of him. He searched my eyes, as if terrified I wouldn't remember him.

"You weren't here." I hated the whine that had sneaked into my voice, but I was hurt, emotionally and physically.

"I'm sorry, Cassie." Hagen's strong hand held mine as he lifted it carefully to kiss the back of it. My eyes had a hard time focusing, but even so, I could see the swelling and scrapes on his knuckles. Had he been in a fight?

"You weren't home," he said, "and I tried calling you. I went to the apartment. There were police everywhere. I saw the blood by your car." He stopped and swallowed hard. "One of your neighbors told me they had taken you in an ambulance, but no one knew which hospital. It took me forever to find you, and I had to call in a favor to get in here with you."

"Kyle called you."

"He didn't." Hagen shook his head as he gently stroked my hand. "Maybe he called the wrong number."

"Maybe."

Hagen started to lift his hand, as if he wanted to stroke my hair as he often did when we were cuddled close together, but he flexed his fingers and lowered them back to the bed. I couldn't see my head, but I could feel the bandages. He carefully trailed his fingertips across my cheek and down my nose toward my mouth. His eyes darkened, and he seemed overcome with emotion. "Oh, baby, what did they do to you?"

"Not they," I corrected, tiredly. "It was Janine."

He seemed taken aback. "Janine?"

"You hurt Travis so she hurt me," I explained, my eyelids drooping again. Feeling myself falling back asleep, I tried to make him understand the situation. "It's your fault."

"Cassie?" He said my name in a voice filled with hurt. "Cassie, that's not true. I didn't do anything to Travis."

"She said you did." Even though I wanted to keep talking to him, to find out the truth, I couldn't stay awake. I fell back into a bottomless chasm of exhaustion and could only hope that Hagen would be next to my bed when I woke up.

He was still there when I woke up—but he wasn't alone.

A nurse with a perky auburn ponytail and a warm smile crouched down next to him, one hand on his thigh and the other holding his hand. It wasn't the kind of touch two strangers would share. It was intimate and familiar.

When Hagen realized I was awake, he drew away from her quickly, standing so fast he almost knocked her back onto her butt. He seemed to realize his mistake as soon as he made it and hurriedly reached down to steady and help her stand. She was tall and not even the utilitarian cut of her scrubs could hide her incredible curves. Laughing softly, she patted him on the back and shook her head. "Easy, John. She's not going anywhere."

With a smile, she walked to the hand sanitizer dispenser on the far wall and waited for a dollop to fill her hands. As she rubbed them together, she introduced herself. "I'm Vicky. I'll be your nurse today. How are you feeling?"

Moving my confused gaze away from Hagen, I winced at the pain in my back and side. "Sore."

"Your head or your body?"

"My body," I clarified.

"You took some nasty hits. The bruising is pretty bad." She checked the IV pump next to the bed and the tubes flowing out of it. "You have a shoe print on your backside."

Upon hearing that detail, Hagen actually grunted. I glanced at him, noticing his stiff jaw and his tightly crossed arms. Anger radiated from him, and I worried he was going to give himself a stroke if he didn't calm down.

"The police were here earlier, but we sent them away. The doctors will be by to do rounds soon, and you'll need some more tests, a CT for sure. If the doctors think you're up to some questioning, we'll let the police in to see you."

I didn't say anything to that. My blurry gaze remained fixed on Hagen, and I wondered if he was sharing my same thoughts about the situation. If I pressed charges against Janine, if I fingered her as the assailant who had beaten me last night, would she turn around and blame Hagen for the attack on Travis? Would both of them end up in jail?

And, anyway, I wasn't sure what the point of pressing charges would be. It wasn't going to rewind the clock and prevent my injuries.

"How does your head feel?" She checked the drainage tube dangling from my bandaged head.

"Okay," I remarked, thinking it was a good sign that my splitting headache had vanished. "There's kind of a throb. Not bad like last night before the surgery."

"Good. Can you rate the pain? On a scale of one to ten?"

"A five," I said after a few seconds of gauging it against the agony of yesterday.

"You have pain meds ordered, and you had a dose right before shift change. You're due for another in, oh, two hours or so, but if the pain increases or you're just super uncomfortable, all you have to do is ask."

Hagen sent me a look that all but begged me to take whatever pain medicine was offered. He clearly couldn't handle the sight of me battered like this.

"So, after rounds and whatever tests they order, you'll get a visit from our traumatic brain injury team," she said as she moved around the bed and checked other tubes leading out of my body from under the blanket. "They're going to want to establish some benchmarks for your current state. You know, checking your language capabilities, your memory recall, things like that."

Knowing she had probably seen more than her fair share of head traumas, I asked, "How bad was it?"

She hesitated at the foot of the bed. "You were lucky, Cassie. Extremely lucky. Being hit like that?" She shook her head.

"You've got some rough weeks ahead of you, but you'll recover well. You'll probably have some lingering side effects, but all the signs so far point to a positive outcome."

Realizing that was the best I was going to get, I nodded and thanked her. She finished her assessment, smiled at us and left with a promise to check in later. Once she was gone, I squinted at the sunlight streaming in through the windows. I didn't even have to ask Hagen to shut the blinds. He moved immediately, making quick work of blocking out the morning sunlight and giving my sensitive eyes a break.

When he was back at my side, he dragged the chair closer and took my hand as he sat. As if he could read my mind, he said, "We dated years ago. Seven years," he clarified. "She wanted to get married and have kids, and I wasn't there yet. She's married. Well," he amended hastily, "divorced actually."

"Okay," I murmured, not at all in the mood to ask uncomfortable questions about it. He seemed to be telling the truth and that was enough for me right now.

"I talked to Ronnie's girlfriend earlier," he said, rubbing his thumb over my hand in slow, soothing strokes. "She said Kyle didn't call her, but he may have tried to reach Ronnie. Your brother just started his fourteen-day shift on the rig, and the service out there is spotty at best. She promised to get a message to him as soon as possible."

"He needs to stay and work. I don't want him messing up his new life because of this. He's safer out there in the middle of the Bering Sea."

"I agree." He adjusted the blanket around my waist. "Is there anything I can get you? They left some water here for you. Do you want to try to drink some?"

"Yes."

Carefully, he held the large plastic tumbler of ice-cold water and guided the straw toward my mouth. I sipped cautiously and swallowed slowly, the fear of bringing it right back up keeping me from gulping down the whole cup to quench my thirst.

"Okay?" He wiped the drip of water from my chin with his thumb.

"Yeah."

He tenderly caressed my cheek, and he seemed overcome with emotion. "Cassie, about Travis, I—"

A knock at the door to my ICU room interrupted us. We both glanced up as a team of doctors entered. Hagen held my hand as the doctors and interns introduced themselves and kept holding it as they discussed my case. A series of tests were ordered as well as evaluations by various therapists.

"We'll compare your scans from last night to the ones we'll get this morning," the head neurologist explained. "Have you ever had an MRI before?"

"A year or so ago," I answered tiredly. "My friend needed another brain for her study."

"Her friend is a neuroscience grad student at Rice," Hagen clarified. "Do you think those scans would be helpful? I'm sure Taylor can get them to you if we ask."

"Actually, they might be," the doctor agreed. "We'll put a call in to Rice and see if we can get them."

I zoned out as Hagen asked more questions, his concern clear as he worried about my vision and memory. Vaguely, I was aware of the doctor telling him the usual spiel about how no two cases are the same and no one really knows what to expect in brain injuries. I wanted to concentrate on the discussion happening, but my mind felt fuzzy and slow, like a bogged down browser that needed a restart.

When the medical team left to see their next patient, I turned toward Hagen's tender and chaste kiss. He stroked my jaw. "Are you okay?"

"Tired," I said with a little yawn. "And sort of confused. My thoughts feel mushy and disjointed."

"Well," he said, the corner of his mouth twitching with amusement, "your vocabulary seems to be just fine." He reached for the tumbler of water on the nearby rolling table and brought the straw to my lips. As I took a small sip, he asked, "How is your vision? Vicky said that you were complaining of double vision and problems on the left side last night."

"Was I?" I couldn't remember—and that scared me. I closed my right eye and realized she was correct. "My left eye is fuzzy."

"Okay, well, we'll get that sorted out," he promised, his voice tinged with fake optimism. "You'll look adorable in glasses," he added with a loving smile.

I wrinkled my nose. "I don't want to be adorable."

"Too late. You already are." He kissed the tip of my nose as if to prove his point. When he sat back, his stomach growled loudly. He made an apologetic face. "Sorry. I missed dinner and breakfast."

"You should go home and shower and have breakfast." I gave Hagen's hand an encouraging squeeze, and he winced a bit, drawing my gaze back down to his hand. The bruising that I had noticed last night was even worse today. "Did you get into a fight?"

"Yes."

I wasn't brave enough to ask if he had fought with Travis. I couldn't even begin to handle the implications of that admission. Like a coward, I ran my fingers over his forearm. "I know you have work and you probably need some sleep. I'll be fine here."

He made a face and shook his head. "I wasn't here last night. I don't want to leave you alone again."

"I won't be alone. I'm surrounded by nurses and doctors. I'll be having tests and evaluations anyway."

He heaved a reluctant sigh and finally relented with a nod. "If anything changes, I'll have them call me."

"Okay."

Hagen carefully leaned toward me and brushed his lips against mine. "I love you."

I cupped his jaw and kissed him. "I love you, too."

After he left, I closed my eyes to rest for a bit. My thoughts were muddled, and my headache was slowly returning. When Vicky returned a while later, she was followed by a pair of techs who took me to the imaging department for the ordered tests. The CT scan went quickly enough, but the thrumming thump of the MRI aggravated my headache. By the time I was returned to my hospital room, I was ready to beg for pain medication.

Thankfully, Vicky seemed to have known I would need something and was waiting with a syringe that went directly into my IV port as soon as I was settled. "You're getting the good stuff today and part of tomorrow, but we'll start to wean you down before you're discharged."

"How long?" I asked, already starting to feel the pain ebbing away as the medication worked its magic. "Before I get discharged?"

"A week, at least," she said and disposed of the syringe in a container mounted on the wall. When she was done, she cleaned her hands and came back to my bedside to check all of the tubes and catheters snaking out of my body. "If you continue to improve, they'll send you to a step-down unit and then out to the regular floor. You want to push yourself to reach the goals they set for you, but you also need to rest. Your body has been through a lot. It needs to recover." She adjusted my blanket and patted my hand. "Why don't you try to nap until lunch? If you need anything, the call button is right here."

Even though it felt as if all I did was sleep, I couldn't keep my eyes open. I drifted off as the pain faded and woke up sometime later to the smell of beef broth. My vision seemed even blurrier as I glanced around the room, and a ball of worry thrummed low in my chest. What if I went blind? What if I could never see the stars again?

"Hey, you're awake." Kyle's voice drew my gaze toward the right side of my bed. He sat in the chair Hagen had earlier vacated. Leaning forward, he put his hand on mine, his face a mask of concern. "You okay?"

"Yeah," I croaked, my throat dry. I tried to adjust the bed, and he hurried over to the controls, helping me settle into a more comfortable and upright position. "Thank you."

"No problem." He gestured toward the rolling table. "They just brought your lunch. Do you want some help with it?"

"Please," I said with a nod.

"Sure. Of course." He pulled the table into place. "Do you want to start with the broth? Or maybe the Jell-O? Or this lemon ice thing?"

"The lemon ice," I decided, my mouth watering as I imagined the taste of it. The reality beat my expectations. My right hand trembled a bit as I spooned the cold lemony ice into my mouth, but I managed not to make a mess. The realization that my body wasn't behaving the way it normally did was hard to accept. Would it always be like this?

"Taylor wanted me to let you know that she's coming by later. She's already got her brother waiting to start your occupational therapy, and Danny gave her a list of speech therapists if you need one." He gestured to the broth or the Jell-O and I pointed toward the Jell-O. As he peeled back the foil lid, he said, "I spoke to Dr. Symonds this morning. She's handling everything school related. She doesn't want you to worry about any of it."

"Thank you, Kyle. I really appreciate that."

"I brought your backpack and phone." He pointed to the empty chair by the window where my backpack now sat. My phone was on the arm of the chair and plugged into the wall to charge. "Your phone was dead, but it's probably got enough battery to make calls or texts."

I grimaced. "There's no way I can handle looking at a screen right now."

"I can send messages if you need help."

"Maybe later," I said, planning to have Hagen help me with that.

Kyle hesitated before asking, "Have the police been here?"

"Apparently, they came earlier but were turned away."

Even with blurry vision, I could read the expression on his face. "Why?"

"They came to see me last night at my apartment. After I'd left here," he clarified. "They told me Travis is in the hospital. This one," he added with a stricken look. "He's down the hall, actually. I don't think he's going to make it."

"What happened?" I wasn't sure I wanted to know, but I couldn't stop myself from asking.

"Someone beat the living shit out of him," Kyle said soberly. "Cracked his head like an egg. I heard the nurses out in the hall talking about the transplant team coming."

"Oh my God." My appetite fled as images of Travis, beaten to a pulp and clinging to life, filtered through my head.

"Cassie," Kyle said forcefully, "they think it was Hagen."

"So did Janine," I admitted before I could stop myself. "That's what she said when she was beating me up, but—"

"But what?"

"Hagen wouldn't do that. He's not that kind of man."

"He's exactly that sort of man," Kyle insisted. "He was a loan shark. I've heard what he was like before he went legitimate. He was violent."

"He may have been what you say, but he's not that man anymore."

"Why? Because of you?" Kyle shook his head. "No, he's not going to let anyone disrespect you. There was no way Travis was walking away from what happened in the laundry room without at least being punched in the face."

I wanted to argue with Kyle. I wanted to tell him he was wrong and Hagen wouldn't do that, but deep down, I had my doubts. He had been ruthless in business and dealt in the seedy underbelly where fists solved most problems. He had never lied to me about any of that. He had always been honest and open about the life he had lived.

"Travis ran with a rough crowd," I countered, unwilling to believe Hagen had done this. "It could have been anyone that hurt him."

"You're here in this hospital bed because the man who loves you fucked up," Kyle said, his voice filled with anger. "You got hurt because of him."

"Kyle, there's no proof this was Hagen's fault."

"The police don't need proof. They need motive—and your man has a ton of it." He frowned down at me. "Don't you understand? Hagen will go to prison. For murder!"

His raised voice made me wince, and I drew back into the bed, pushing against the lumpy pillow tucked behind me. Kyle breathed heavily as he scowled at me, seemingly overcome with frustration as I refused to think the worst of Hagen.

"Is everything okay?" Vicky asked from the doorway, her worried gaze darting from me to Kyle.

"Yes," I said, not taking my eyes off Kyle. "My friend was just leaving."

"I'm sorry," Kyle said immediately. "I'm sorry, Cassie. I shouldn't have upset you. I'm just trying to look out for you."

"I know you are." Not wanting to argue, I said, "But I'm tired. I'd like to nap."

"Sure. Right," he said quietly, awkwardly. "I'll, uh, I'll check in with you tomorrow."

Vicky kept an eye on him as he crossed the hospital room and left. Once he was gone, she walked over to my bedside and looked me over. "Are you okay?"

"Yes. He's just trying to look out for me."

"Uh-huh," she replied, unconvinced. "If Hagen knew he was in here shouting at you like that…"

I met her knowing gaze and felt the unwanted pang of jealousy. Had Hagen defended her once? Had he protected her? Saved her? Had he loved her? Had he done with her what he did with me? Used his hands and mouth to bring her to wild peaks of pleasure that left her panting and boneless and utterly and completely overwhelmed by love for him?

"The therapists are here to do their evaluations," she said, breaking into my troubled thoughts. "Do you want me to ask them to come back later?"

"No." I was desperate for a distraction. "I'm fine."

I'm not fine. Not even a little bit.

CHAPTER SEVEN

SORE AND UNCOMFORTABLE, I adjusted the bed and tried to find a position that didn't make my back hurt. Just when I thought I had finally found it, someone knocked on my door. I sighed and then inwardly groaned as two police officers walked into the room.

"Hi, Cassie," the female officer greeted. "I'm Officer Delgado and this is Officer Greene. Is it okay if we come in and chat for a bit?"

"Um, sure, I guess," I replied uncertainly.

"Great." Officer Delgado smiled as she shut the door behind them. "How are you feeling?"

"Like someone drilled a hole in my head," I said matter-of-factly.

Officer Greene chuckled. "I bet you do."

"So," Officer Delgado said as she pulled up a chair, "we were able to get your clothing from the ER last night. It will be processed for evidence. We also have some statements from neighbors who saw the assault. Do you think you could walk us through what happened?"

I took a deep breath and told them everything I could remember. From the questions Officer Greene asked, it was clear they knew all the details except for what Janine said to me. I hesitated before telling them, not wanting to implicate Hagen in the attack on Travis.

"Do you think that's what happened?" Officer Delgado asked.

"That Hagen attacked Travis over a laundry basket? No. Of course not," I insisted. "He's not going to risk jail over ten dollars."

"Maybe it wasn't about the baskets," Officer Greene suggested. "Maybe it was about sending a message that no one disrespects his girl."

"No. Hagen wouldn't do that. That's not who he is."

"You sure about that?" Officer Delgado asked.

"Yes." Not in the mood for any more questions about Hagen, I said, "Can we wrap this up? My head is killing me, and I just want to sleep."

"Sure. Sorry," she apologized. "We need some photos of your injuries if that's okay?"

"That's fine."

Officer Greene stepped out of the room to get Vicky. She helped the officers shift me onto my side to get photos of the bruises on my back and bottom as well as clear shots of the bandaged wound on my head. When they were finished, they placed a business card on the rolling cart and left.

"You okay?" Vicky asked as she rearranged my pillows and straightened out my various IV and drain lines.

"Yes."

"I think you should ask for no visitors tonight and tomorrow. You need to rest. You've had people in and out all day. I think you would benefit from some uninterrupted quiet and sleep." She tucked the blanket around my waist. "I can tell

Hagen when he comes and have him let your friends know that you need to rest."

"Okay," I said, trying to stifle a yawn. "Can he stay the night?"

"That chair reclines." She gestured to the chair closer to the wall. "It won't be comfortable, and it's too short for him, but he'll survive." She pulled the rolling tray closer to my bed so I could reach the water if I wanted it. "Do you need anything else?"

"No."

"We are about to start shift change. Ameka, your night nurse, will come in and introduce herself and give your next dose of pain meds. She's really great. You'll be in good hands."

Smiling at her, I watched her leave the room and then sagged into the pillows propping me up in the uncomfortable bed. Exhaustion overwhelmed me, and I dozed off again. It seemed as if my eyes had been closed only a minute when I was awoken by a slight tug on my IV. I gazed, bleary-eyed, at the new nurse at my left side.

"Sorry, hon, I didn't mean to wake you," she apologized quietly. "I'm Ameka. I'm your nurse tonight." She tapped at the touchscreen monitor next to my bed, updating my record, and then scanned the barcode on the capped syringe in her hand. "These are your pain meds. How are you feeling now? On a scale of one-to-ten?"

"A six, I guess," I answered uncertainly. My head was pounding, the thud deep and harsh as it caused my stomach to churn with nausea. "Can I have something to settle my stomach?"

"Of course," Ameka replied quickly. "You have orders for

anti-nausea meds. Would you like me to get rid of this dinner tray?"

"If I could just get something to drink, I'll be fine," I said, the idea of any kind of food making the nausea even worse. The scent of the broth that had tasted so good at lunch now made me want to gag. "Something cold," I added. "Please."

"Okay." She placed the juice and Sprite that had come with my dinner tray on the rolling cart and covered up the other things I didn't want. Tray in hand, she said, "Let me grab those meds, and I'll be right back."

As the pain medication started to flatten the pounding throb in my head, I closed my eyes and breathed slowly, desperate to ease the nausea rolling through my stomach. The door opened, but I kept my eyes closed, feeling that awful mouthwatering panic starting to build. Not wanting to vomit, certain it was going to make my head feel even worse, I tried to will away the sensation but it was useless.

"Cassie!" Hagen was suddenly at my side, a pink basin in one hand as he gently supported me with the other. "It's okay, baby. Just let it out."

Embarrassed and in pain, I made a mess of the basin, the meager lunch I had eaten coming up in a puddle. "I'm sorry."

"There's no reason to apologize." He rubbed my back and held the basin in place. "Is that all?"

"I think so."

As I closed my eyes, he guided me back to the pillows. His heavy footsteps marked his trip to the bathroom to deal with the basin and then his walk back to my bedside. He had a warm, wet cloth in his hand that he used to wipe my face. "Better?"

"Yes," I answered, my voice raspy and weak.

"Drink some water, baby," he urged, holding a straw to my lips with his bruised hands. I didn't want to drink anything, but I knew he was right. I needed to stay hydrated. He dabbed at my mouth again with the cloth and set aside the cup of water. "Are the pain meds bothering your stomach?"

"Maybe?" I swallowed thickly. "My nurse is getting some anti-nausea medication for me."

"Good." He stroked my cheek, and I leaned into his touch, soothed by his warm skin on mine. "I wish this bed was bigger so I could climb in and hold you."

His rough voice and the vulnerable softness to his eyes made my heart flutter. I reached out to touch his jaw—and then a horrible screech broke us apart. A commotion erupted in the hallway as a woman shouted and others tried to calm her down. She didn't react well to that, and a second later, the crash of metal clanged loudly. The door to my room flew open, and Hagen rose to his full height, spinning toward the door and blocking my body with his.

I couldn't see the woman who ran shrieking into my hospital room, but I could hear her. She was completely out of control as she screamed, "You're the son-of-a-bitch who killed my son!"

All hell broke loose as the woman rushed Hagen, battering him with her fists and trying to claw at his face. She was too short to do much damage, and he twisted away from the hospital bed, putting as much distance between her and me as possible. The woman—Travis's mother, I assumed—was enraged, spewing angry words as she attacked Hagen. Even though he easily could have shoved her away or knocked her down, Hagen only blocked her blows.

"Ma'am! Please!" A doctor tried to grab her, but she smacked his hands away and lurched at Hagen again, this time swinging the chair at him like a TV wrestler. Soon, other doctors and nurses were in the room, all of them trying to get a handle on her. Ameka skirted along the edge of the altercation and stood in front of me, taking up the same spot Hagen had been in earlier, protecting me from any wayward blows. Finally, a pair of security guards ran into the room and managed to get a hold of her.

"You little bitch! I know it was your fault! You and your lowlife brother!" She kicked and screamed, cursing me and Hagen as they dragged her out of the room. Her voice echoed down the hallway as she called us murderers and vowed to kill us.

Shocked by the scene, I sat there, mouth agape, heart racing, and tried not to cry. I couldn't find it in myself to be mad at her. She was a grieving mother, desperate for answers and for somewhere to place the blame.

"Are you okay?" Hagen strode toward me, his eyes stormy as he brushed off the concerns of the doctor and nurse who were trying to tend to his scratched neck and forearms.

"I'm okay. Are you?" I reached for him and let my gaze roam over his body, taking in the scratches and bruises already developing.

"I'm so sorry," the doctor apologized. "That shouldn't have happened."

"You're damn right it shouldn't have happened," Hagen snapped angrily. "I spoke to your staff about this before I left this morning. I warned them something like this could happen if their visitors weren't kept separate."

The doctor raised his hands in a silent gesture to placate Hagen. "We were keeping them separate, but Travis's case was..." He trailed off as if realizing he was stumbling right into a HIPAA violation. "The situation changed this afternoon, and there were no more visitors expected."

I glanced at Hagen, catching his gaze as understanding registered. Looking at the doctor, I said, "We aren't going to hold the hospital liable, and we aren't going to press charges or cause any problems for her. Please make sure she's able to go home and grieve."

The doctor nodded and left the room, taking the extra nurses with him. Ameka washed her hands and checked me over again. She trailed her fingers along the IV lines and the tubes coming out of my head drain before giving me the dose of meds for the nausea. She made a note that I had vomited and then left me the room, quietly closing the door behind her.

Hagen had disappeared into the bathroom while she was assessing me. He came out with his face and arms freshly scrubbed, the scratches cleaned and the blood rinsed away. He dropped into the chair next to my bed, exhaling roughly and leaning forward with his head in his hands. "What a fucking shit show this is."

My gaze lingered on his scraped and swollen knuckles. I didn't want to go there. I really didn't. But I couldn't help but wonder if he wasn't telling me the truth. Travis's mother's voice echoed in my head, her accusations that Hagen had killed him leaving me to question if something had actually happened.

"John."

He looked up, his eyes narrowing when he saw the serious expression on my face. "Yeah?"

I swallowed anxiously. "What happened to your hands?"

"I told you." His eyes flicked away from my face for just a second. "I was in a fight."

"With?"

"It doesn't matter."

"It does." I studied him for a moment before finding the courage to ask, "Did you fight with Travis?"

He looked down, as if he couldn't bear to meet my gaze. Scrubbing his hands through his hair, he blew out a noisy breath and admitted, "Yes, but—"

"But what?" My stomach clenched with panic. "Did you beat him? Did you hurt him?"

"I punched him. Twice."

"Oh my God." I covered my face with my hands as the horror of our situation hit me.

"No. No!" Hagen sat forward and reached for my hands, drawing them away from my face. "I didn't hit him that hard. He came into the bar, spewing his fucking nonsense, looking for a fight. I warned him to go, but he started running his mouth about you, and I snapped. But he walked away from the bar."

"Did he hit his head? Did he fall? Are you sure he walked away? He wasn't stumbling or dizzy or…?"

"Jesus Christ, Cassie! Are you seriously asking me that?"

"You lied to me about the fight. Of course, I'm asking you this. Did. You. Kill. Him?"

"No!"

I flinched at his raised voice. "Don't shout at me."

Shamefaced, he nodded. "I didn't hurt him bad enough to kill him, Cassie. You have to believe me."

"What I believe isn't the issue, John. His mother thinks you did. Has she told the police that? Are they going to find witnesses who saw you two fighting?"

"They can question anyone they like. Everyone will vouch for me."

"And Janine?"

"What about her?"

"She tried to bash in my skull in last night because she thought you were the one who put Travis in the hospital!"

"This isn't my fault!"

My head pounded as our argument grew heated. "Yes, it is!"

He jerked back as if I had slapped him. "Is that what you think?"

"I don't know what to think anymore." I gritted my teeth and fought the tears burning my eyes. I was on edge and barely able to contain my emotions. "I tried to stop you from confronting them in the laundry room, but you stormed off and had to handle things the way you always do. You got into a fight with Travis. He ends up in the hospital where he dies. Janine attacked me, and now I'm here, with a hole in my head and blood on my brain. I might end up with permanent brain damage. I could develop seizures or never recover the vision in my eye."

"What are you saying, Cassie?"

I looked away from him, his chest heaving as he breathed and gritted his teeth, and wiped at the tears running down my face. "I don't know what I'm saying."

"I think you do," he said angrily and stood. "If that's what you think, if you intend to blame me for what happened to you, then I should leave."

My heart broke, and I couldn't bear to lift my gaze to his. "Maybe you should."

He hesitated only a second before striding out of my hospital room without another word.

Crushed, I closed my eyes and leaned back against the pillow. Carefully, so as not to disturb my IV or the drainage tubes, I turned away from the door and let the tears come.

CHAPTER EIGHT

W HEN THERE WAS a timid knock at my hospital room door the next morning, I turned my hopeful gaze toward it. A moment later, Kyle poked his head into the room, and I had to school my features to keep my disappointment from showing. It wasn't his fault that I was expecting Hagen.

Kyle didn't seem to notice and smiled contritely. "May I come inside?"

"Sure. Of course."

He carried in a green glass vase filled with bright, happy sunflowers and a small gift bag. As he placed the vase on the counter across from the hospital bed, he said, "I wanted to apologize for the way I behaved yesterday." He moved to the empty chair next to my bed and sighed. "I only want what's best for you. I want you to be safe. I shouldn't have upset you like that."

"I appreciate your apology." My gaze moved to the pretty sunflowers cheering up my room. "And the flowers."

"I saw them in the shop, and it reminded me of the photos of you and Taylor at the corn maze last year. You had your faces in those big wooden sunflower photo props."

"That was a fun day," I said, a little surprised he remembered those photos we had shared on Instagram. "I had planned to take Hagen next weekend, but after last night…"

Kyle frowned. "After last night what?"

I shrugged. "It's complicated."

"I have time. I'm here to listen if you want to talk." He smiled encouragingly. "I've had plenty of experience with peer counseling. Let me help you."

I wasn't sure I was ready for that just yet. It seemed like a violation of my relationship with Hagen to tell Kyle about our fight. Part of that was me wanting to protect Hagen from anyone thinking less of him. I didn't want my friends to hold grudges against him.

"We were both stressed out last night and said some things we shouldn't have," I explained. "We'll figure it out."

If he comes back…

"If there's anything I can do to help, just ask."

"I will." I couldn't imagine what Kyle could do to help fix a problem with my boyfriend, but it was nice of him to offer nonetheless.

"Here." Kyle handed me the small gift bag. "I got you something as an apology-slash-get-well present."

"You didn't have to get me something," I protested. "Flowers were more than enough."

"I wanted to," he insisted. "Open it."

Curious, I pulled out the bunched-up sheets of pink tissue paper and reached into the bag to retrieve the bracelet inside. The round enamel beads were a brilliant blue with white circles and black dots on each one. With my vision still blurry in one eye, it was hard to examine the beads, but they seemed to be hand painted. One had a little defect in the black paint, just a little scuff that made the bracelet all that more precious.

"Oh, it's so pretty!"

"It's supposed to be a Russian good luck charm. Something about repelling the Evil Eye."

"God knows I need all the luck I can get lately," I murmured and carefully slid the bracelet onto my wrist. I enjoyed the look the of the blue beads against my skin. "Thank you, Kyle. It's so sweet."

"You're very welcome." He tucked the paper back in the bag and placed the bag on the rolling table. "So, how are you feeling this morning?"

"Tired," I admitted. "Sore. I have a headache, but it's not too bad."

"Is that going to be a long-term thing? The headaches, I mean?"

"Maybe," I replied uncertainly. "The neuro team told me that it's hard to predict what head injuries will do. I'm lucky that mine was minor, all things considered."

"Doesn't seem very minor to me," he grumbled. "You had to have your head drilled open."

"Yes, but I didn't have a stroke or lose a huge chunk of my brain function," I reasoned.

"Your vision? Has that cleared up any?"

"No," I answered reluctantly.

He sighed. "I'm sorry, Cassie."

"It will get better," I said, more to convince myself than him.

"When do you think they'll let you out of here?"

"No idea. I probably have another five to seven days here."

He made a face. "Seven days of hospital food."

"Surprisingly, it's not so bad. It's nothing like the cafeteria garbage we all ate as kids."

"If you need me to sneak in some Whataburger or a couple of tacos, let me know."

"I'll probably take you up on that offer once they move me to the step-down unit."

"When is that happening?"

"The doctors did their rounds earlier and think I should be able to move there tomorrow."

"Will you be going back to your apartment when they discharge you?"

"I'm moving in with Hagen." A little uncertain, I ran my fingers over the cold enamel beads of the bracelet. "Or, at least, I was."

Kyle hesitated before offering, "My second bedroom is still available if you need a place to land for a bit."

"I'll keep that in mind." I wasn't sure that was a viable option either. I would need help the first few days out of the hospital, especially with showering, and there was no way I was going to ask a guy friend to help with that. I wasn't even sure I would feel comfortable asking Taylor for that kind of help, but if Hagen was still upset with me, I wouldn't have much choice.

Kyle checked his watch. "I have to run, but if you need anything, just call or have one of the nurses help you text me, okay? I'm scheduled to volunteer at the counseling center later, but I can leave if something comes up."

"Taylor is coming by later, but thanks."

"No worries." He stood up and moved closer to give me a hug. It was a bit awkward with all of my IV lines and bandages, and his arm got tangled up in the drain dangling from the side of my head. "Sorry, Cassie."

We laughed as we untangled everything, and I was still smiling when he left. The smile and happiness didn't last long. Alone with my thoughts, I let my gaze drift to my phone. It had been sitting next to me on the bed all morning but had yet to ring or chirp with a message notification. Tired of waiting, I decided to reach out first, hoping Hagen was ready to talk.

I covered my left eye to clear up my blurry vision and tapped at the screen. I had to stop and delete so many times because my fingers were fumbling. Even when I managed to type things correctly, I couldn't stand to look at the screen for more than a few seconds at a time. My stomach swirled with nausea, and I hoped I wasn't going to throw up again. My short message typed and sent, I dropped my phone back on the bed and closed my eyes, leaning back against the pillows and willing my stomach to stop pitching.

"Hagen stopping by soon?" Vicky asked as she brought in my next dose of meds and checked my IVs and the drain.

"I'm not sure," I answered, not at all in the mood to talk about Hagen with her. She seemed to understand I wasn't looking to chat and finished her work without another word.

After she left, I turned onto my side and decided to sleep. Fatigue seemed to have settled into my very bones, drawing out all the strength I had and leaving me so tired I could barely stay awake for more than a couple of hours at a time. The neuro team had warned me that I would need more sleep than usual for the next few months, but I hadn't realized they meant this kind of exhaustion. It was unsettling and left me feeling weak and vulnerable.

A long time later, I woke to the smell of a dinner tray. The scent turned my stomach, and even though it was so empty it growled, I couldn't bear the thought of trying to eat anything on the tray. It was still sitting there untouched when Taylor arrived.

"You need to eat." She lifted the lid on the tray and scanned the offerings. "The chicken soup looks good."

"Then you can eat it," I replied snappishly.

Her eyebrows arched. "Wow, they must have skipped your anti-bitch pills today."

I rolled my eyes before apologizing. "Sorry."

She put the lid back on the tray and sat on the edge of the bed. "Spill it. Tell me what's got you so cranky." When I didn't immediately talk, she poked my leg. "Hagen?"

I nodded and swallowed hard.

"Did he get busy at work and not make it in yet?"

I shook my head.

"Cassie, this is going to take forever if you make me keep guessing."

I blinked back tears. "We had a fight last night."

"A fight? Here? While you're in a fucking hospital bed with a hole in your head? What the hell is wrong with him?"

"It wasn't just him. I accused him of something awful, and he got upset." I rubbed my forehead and sighed. "It was a mess."

"And he hasn't come back since he left last night?"

"No."

"He didn't call or text or anything?" She picked up my phone as if to check for herself.

"No."

"Asshole," she muttered. "Do you want me to go find him

and drag him back here? Because I will. I may have to get Danny to help because Hagen is such a giant, but I'll get him in here if you want him."

"No, if he needs time, I should let him have it."

"What about what you need?"

Her question broke the dam holding back my tears. Even though it made my head pound to cry, I couldn't stop. I sobbed as Taylor hugged me close and soothingly rubbed my back. What I needed and wanted was Hagen.

And I seemed to have pushed him away, maybe for good.

CHAPTER NINE

"ARE YOU SURE you don't want to take my bed?" Taylor asked for the fifth time since moving me into her apartment earlier that day.

"I'm sure." Gesturing to the chair recliner where I planned to sleep, I explained, "I feel better when I'm upright. It's how I slept in the hospital."

"Okay," she said uncertainly. "But, if you change your mind, just wake me up, and we'll switch."

"Sure," I agreed, knowing she wouldn't rest unless I promised.

"And if you get sick, just yell."

"I will."

"And if you need anything—a glass of water or a snack or medicine—just yell."

"Taylor," I laughed, "go to sleep. I'll be fine."

She clearly didn't believe me and reluctantly left the living room. When she was at her bedroom door, she called out, "I'm leaving my door open so I can hear you if you need help!"

I snorted. "Okay. Thanks."

Grateful to have such a good friend, I switched off the lamp in the corner and settled into the recliner. After eight days in the hospital, it was an absolute relief to be able to sit in a dark, cool place without the constant beep of machines in the background or well-meaning nurses waking me when they came into the room to check my IV or give me medicine. I sunk back into the plush chair and exhaled slow, deep breaths, letting the exhaustion I felt overwhelm me and drag me closer to sleep.

But the nagging, painful replay of Hagen walking out on me, leaving me alone in the hospital to never return, wouldn't let me rest. My injured brain seemed intent on torturing me with the memory of his broad shoulders disappearing through the door. No phone calls. Not even a text. He had just left. He had ended everything without another word.

Not wanting to cry again, knowing it would give me a headache and make me nauseated, I managed to breathe through the gut-wrenching emotional pain and turn my thoughts toward other things. Because I had ended my lease, I had no place to go. Kyle had packed up my place for me and stored my things at his until I could find somewhere else. He had offered, again, to let me move into his second bedroom, but I couldn't stand the sight of the complex. I didn't want to live somewhere that would force me to relive the memory of being beaten every time I walked out into the parking lot.

Staying with Taylor was the best solution for now. She had a lead on a sublet that another grad student needed was advertising. It was within my price range, close to campus and a block's walk from the METRO Red Line that ran toward Rice. If I could snag it, I could move in and get settled by the end of the week. Hopefully.

And then I could start the grueling process of moving on.

Moving on from my injury. Moving on from the failure of

my relationship. Moving on toward the future that awaited me in California or Massachusetts.

I slept better that night in Taylor's living room than I had since my injury. Feeling well-rested, I woke up before Taylor and folded my blanket and tucked it under the pillow. I made sure the space I was borrowing was tidy before carefully making my way to the bathroom. I tried to be as quiet as possible while Taylor snoozed in her bedroom. I had already put my clothes for the day and my toiletries in her bathroom the night prior so I wouldn't have to make much noise.

After I showered and got dressed, I emerged from the bathroom to find her sitting up in bed, staring at her phone. "Morning."

"Morning," she said, smiling at me. "You know," she stretched her arms overhead and yawned, "I think we should egg his house. Like toilet paper, eggs, shaving cream—the whole shebang. Just fuck his place right up."

The idea of working out my anger toward Hagen with a little juvenile vandalism held some appeal. Still, there was a chance that he might come back and make things right so I said, "Let's table that for now."

She pouted. "Fine."

"Can you help brush out my hair?" It felt silly to have to ask for help doing something I had been able to handle since I was a child. "My arms are still weak, and I can't feel the wound very well. It's numb all around it, and I don't want to accidentally grab the stitches."

"Dude," she said and held out her hand for the comb and brush I carried, "get over here and let me help you."

I settled onto the bed in front of her, and she began to gently comb through my tangled and matted hair. The blood, bandages and electrode gel used to monitor my brain had made an absolute mess of my hair. Taylor had helped me wash it the night before they discharged me, but we didn't dare try to comb it without plenty of conditioner on hand.

"Good call leaving in the conditioner," she said while tugging the comb through the ends of my hair. "There's a mat closer to your stitches that I'm going to leave alone. I don't want to pull and make you bleed."

"I guess we should go to Target and find a few hats for me to wear out in public," I said, trying to make light of the situation.

"Not a bad idea," she agreed, working her way through the next section of hair. "Do you want me to check your phone for messages from Hagen?"

Since I couldn't focus on any kind of screen without getting dizzy and wanting to hurl, Taylor had been the one to send a few messages to Hagen for me. One had been to see when he was coming back to the hospital the day following our argument. The other had been to let him know I was being discharged. The final one had been to let him know I was staying at Taylor's place for now. None had been answered or even read.

"Sure."

"Do you want me to send him another message for you? Or maybe call?"

"No," I said eventually. "I've reached out multiple times. It's his turn."

She moved the comb through another section of my hair. "How long are you going to wait before you decide it's really over?"

"A few more days, I guess," I replied uncertainly. "But I think we both know it's done."

She paused combing to squeeze my shoulder. "I never thought he would do you like this. I always thought he was an old-school sort of gentleman, you know?"

"I know," I murmured quietly.

She worked on the snarls near the back of my head for a few minutes. "Do you think he was responsible for Travis's death?"

"No," I said after a while. "I think Hagen did fight him earlier in the day, but something else must have happened to Travis after that."

"Someone else," she corrected. "God only knows how many enemies he had."

"Hagen, too."

"You think someone tried to frame Hagen for Travis's murder?"

"It's possible, right? I mean, his business is all legitimate now, but it wasn't always. He still has friends who aren't exactly the city's most upstanding citizens."

I didn't name the men I was thinking of—Besian Beciraj or that scary ass Russian Kostya. I had only met the Russian once and that was frankly enough. Besian, however, I had seen a few times at Hagen's place. The two were old friends and enjoyed playing cards together.

"I could see someone trying to frame him," she agreed, "but I don't even want to imagine what sort of crazy asshole would do that." She tugged the comb through the last of a snarl. "Do you think it's someone you know?"

"I hope not." I shuddered at the thought that someone was creeping around, waiting to hurt me or Hagen again.

"Do you want me to…," she trailed off as if she wasn't quite sure how to finish it. "Do you want me to go to Hagen's place and pick up your things?"

The thought of Taylor going to the house that was supposed to be my new home and boxing up my belongings made my eyes burn. A ball of emotion clogged my throat, and I had to swallow down the thick pain of it, refusing to cry again. "No. Not…not yet."

"Okay." She set aside the comb and picked up the brush. As she drew the bristles through my detangled hair, she asked, "What's on the schedule for today?"

Glad for the change of subject, I said, "Neurosurgeon follow-up appointment at ten, meeting the new neurologist at eleven and then my occupational therapy intake appointment at one."

"You'll like Danny's clinic." Her older brother was the occupational therapist who had agreed to take me on as a client. He worked in a clinic not far from the university and on the same METRO line that I would be using. "He can be a hard ass, but he's only tough because he wants his clients to get better."

"I'll try to remember that."

"If he's really mean to you, tell me and I'll thump him the next time I see him," she promised.

I laughed. "Okay."

"I think if we pull this into a loose, messy bun, no one will be able to see the wound." She gently wound my hair up and held it in place with her hand. "Or I could braid it to one side?"

"Let's leave it down until my appointment with the neurologist. He's probably going to want poke around over there."

"Ugh," she huffed dramatically. "I'll have to leave the room if they're going to clip these stitches. I literally barfed all over my mom when I had to have stitches clipped out of my arm when I was eleven."

"Your poor mom!"

"Eh, she's a nurse. She's been yakked on by hundreds of people." Taylor finished brushing my hair. "Okay. You're done. Now—scoot! I'm about to do the potty dance like a preschooler."

As she dashed off to the bathroom, I gathered up my brush and comb and walked over to the suitcase I had set up in the corner of her room. I found the pair of socks I wanted and made my way to the kitchen to take my morning medications. The low throb in the back of my head was starting to return, and I knew it would get worse as the day wore on and I moved around more. I had never been a particularly religious person, but God, if I didn't pray the headaches would go away soon. They were exhausting and frustrating, and I didn't know how many more days and weeks of this I could stand.

"Cereal?" Taylor asked as she swept into the kitchen in her bathrobe with her wet hair wound up in a towel. "Or something heavier like eggs?"

I made a face at the idea of eggs and gestured to the box of oatmeal on the counter. Kyle had taken all of the food I had packed into my car the night of my attack and made sure all of the pantry goods had been brought to Taylor's place. The refrigerated and frozen things had all gone bad before he could get to them. "I'll make some oatmeal."

"You eat your old lady gruel. I'm having a big ass bowl of *Lucky Charms*."

"You'll be hungry in an hour," I warned.

"Which is exactly perfect because we'll stop for breakfast tacos on the way to your first appointment," she decided with a grin.

I grabbed a packet of oatmeal from the box and some milk from the refrigerator. Taylor handed me a bowl and spoon, and I moved to the microwave to make my breakfast. As she walked around behind me, making her coffee and pouring out her giant serving of cereal, unbidden memories of Hagen sharing kitchen space with me—at his place and mine—flashed before my eyes. It had always felt so easy and simple with him, so naturally domestic and right.

Would I ever hear his deep, soothing voice? Feel his strong hands on my body? Tremble under his talented mouth as he did wicked, dirty things to me in his bed?

The resounding coldness of the answer to those questions settled low in my belly.

No.

CHAPTER TEN

"CASSIE, TAKE A deep breath and try again," Danny urged in his calm, encouraging way.

I shot Taylor's older brother an annoyed look as the timer on the game ticked away the remaining seconds. I hated *Perfection*. The stupid little shapes and the outrageously small spots where they fit were hard enough to figure out when I was in perfect health. Now, with my wonky vision and hand weakness on my left side, I was about to lose my shit trying to make the pieces fit.

The timer dinged, and the game jumped, scattering the pieces I hadn't managed to slide into place correctly. With a huff of frustration, I dropped back against the hard plastic chair and fought the impulse to sweep the whole damn thing off the table and onto the floor. "I really hate this part of our sessions."

"I know you do." Danny made some notes on his iPad. "I know this is hard for you, but the work you're doing is already showing improvements. Your scores are already climbing."

"Not fast enough," I growled, glaring at my offending hand.

"You can't fix this overnight, Cassie. It's going to take time. Weeks. Months," he said, setting aside his tablet. "You will regain your hand strength and coordination."

"And my eye?"

"That's a question for your ophthalmologist," he reasoned. "We're doing the exercises she suggested. You're patching your eye, right?"

I nodded. "I look ridiculous wearing that thing."

"If you were one of my younger clients, I'd help you bedazzle it or turn it into a pirate patch," he teased.

"Taylor tried to convince me to let her go Pinterest crazy on it."

"That sounds like something my sister would suggest," he replied with a smile. "There are other options for your eye. I'm sure the doctor talked to you about them."

I nodded again. "Glasses, Botox and surgery, but the thought of having a needle anywhere near my eyeball makes me want to hurl," I admitted.

"They give you the good drugs before they start working on your eyes," Danny assured me. "I had Lasix done on my eyes a few years ago. I was zonked out of my gourd by the time they started the surgery." He glanced at his watch. "I think we have time to run through some hand stretches before you leave."

Once the stretches were done, he handed out my homework for the weekend. It was more of the same—memory games, patching my good eye, mazes, puzzles, hand exercises and stretching. As I left his office, I slipped on a pair of sunglasses and zipped up my well-worn hoodie. The walk down to the METRO stop wasn't far, and I slowly shrugged my shoulders to release the pent-up tension.

I didn't like failing. I didn't like not being able to master something on the first or second try. Sitting through my therapy sessions was absolute torture. Being forced to acknowledge my new shortcomings was painful. Being forced to accept that my life might never be the same was terrifying.

The friendships I had formed during my years at Rice were the only thing keeping me going these days. Taylor, Kunal and Kyle had stepped up in a huge way, ferrying me back and forth to appointments, helping me move into the little sublet and keeping me company in the evenings when I tended to get a bit maudlin. Classmates offered their notes or study sessions. My professors had all made any accommodations necessary to help me finish my degree.

Kyle had helped me get established with a counselor at the center on campus where he volunteered. I hadn't been keen on the idea at first. Taylor finally convinced me I was being ridiculous and pointed out that the university would be more likely to give me all the accommodations I needed with class and work if I was using the on-campus services. So far, it had been nice to have someone to talk to without judgment.

While I appreciated the care and concern of my friends, it was Hagen's concern and care I yearned for more than anything. Taking my seat on the METRO, I fought the urge to pull out my phone, to cover my left eye and check my messages. It had been almost four weeks since he walked out on me, leaving me alone in the hospital after our argument. Four weeks—and not a single word.

Not wanting to believe that he would end things so cruelly and coldly, I had been seized with the idea that he was in trouble. Had he been arrested for Travis's murder? Was he being held without bail? Did he need help?

I had checked all the news outlets and the daily arrest reports. I even called HPD and the Harris County Sheriff to make sure he wasn't being held. He wasn't. And, when the two officers who had visited me in the hospital followed up with me, I had asked them if they had any suspects in Travis's death. They had mentioned clearing Hagen, and that was the moment I knew he had turned his back on me and given up on us.

A few days later, Kyle had showed up at the door of my new apartment with a stack of boxes. They had been waiting on his doorstep and were labeled with my name in handwriting I would recognize anywhere. Apparently, not knowing where I was and not wanting to speak with me ever again, Hagen had boxed up all my things at his place and dumped them on Kyle's welcome mat. It was the final nail in our relationship coffin.

Yet I couldn't stop thinking about him. I played our last conversation on a loop in my head, trying to figure out where it had all gone wrong. Looking back, I could understand how hurt Hagen must have been that I doubted him or thought him capable of murder. At the same time, he had lied to me about the bruises on his hands. What else was I supposed to think?

It didn't matter anymore, I supposed. It was done. Over. Finished. The promise of the future we had together had been blown up by ruined laundry, of all the stupid things. That one ridiculous event had caused a ripple effect of bad decisions that ended with Travis dead, Janine on the run, and me recovering from a brain injury. It was a total shit show.

I tried to enjoy the cooler, dryer fall weather as I walked

from my stop to the tiny studio I was renting. It was in an even older complex than the one I had been living in earlier, but it was filled with young families and graduate students. I had purged even more of my things after moving, donating, selling and trashing what I could to pare down to the necessities.

Exhausted from a long day at the university and my therapy session and walks, I dropped down on the love seat I had decided to keep. I tossed my backpack aside, not caring where it landed. The moment I closed my eyes and tilted back my head, the low, pounding thump of pain that seemed to always be with me grew more insistent. I blew out an angry breath and tried to relax.

The headaches seemed to be the one side effect that hadn't gotten better. The neurologist handling my case had warned me they could last for months. I had bottles of medications that were supposed to help, but none of them did much. So far, caffeine seemed to be the most helpful. Quiet, dark spaces, too.

But the problem with sitting quietly in a dark space was that the peace never lasted long. Intrusive thoughts would bombard me, and I would slide into a pit of melancholy and worry. What would happen to me if I never got my vision back? If the headaches never went away? If my memory didn't continue to improve? Would I be able to finish a doctorate? Would I be able to find a job?

My phone chimed, and for once, I was grateful for the interruption. I still had a hard time reading text on any sort of screen right now. All of my friends knew to call or video chat with me. Kyle's smiling face came into view after I swiped the screen. "Hey, Kyle."

"Hey! Are you busy later? I thought I might swing by and pick you up for dinner? Or coffee?"

"Coffee sounds nice." I still had random bouts of nausea and wasn't ready to attempt eating in a restaurant where the smells and sounds aggravated my stomach. "What time?"

"Eight? Or is that too late?"

"No, that's perfect."

"Great. I'll see you then."

"Yep."

I closed my left eye so I could focus on my phone and set an alarm. Tired, I dragged myself off the loveseat and walked the handful of steps to my downsized twin bed. Lately, sleeping in clothing had felt uncomfortable and irritating so I had taken to skipping pajamas altogether. The only perk of living alone was that I could sleep however I liked without worrying about anyone else seeing me naked.

As I crawled into bed and pulled the covers over my body, I slid my hand under one of my pillows and stopped when I felt the slightly stiff fabric hidden away there. I slowly pulled free the shirt I had squirreled away under the pillow. It was the only piece of Hagen left in my life, a crisp white dress shirt that still smelled of his cologne and aftershave. In a moment of embarrassing weakness, I held the shirt to my nose and breathed in deeply. The scent was fading now, and I knew that soon it would smell of nothing. But, right now, in this moment, it was the comfort I needed to make it through another day.

When my alarm woke me later, I felt better, a little more rested and without that frustratingly strong thud of a headache. Very carefully, I folded Hagen's shirt and replaced it under the pillow, hiding it away like the shameful secret it was. Clearing my mind of all thoughts of him, I changed into something more comfortable—leggings and an oversized Rice University hoodie over a t-shirt—and waited for Kyle to knock.

"Ready?" he asked when I opened the door.

Nodding, I locked up and followed him to his waiting car. I settled into the front seat and buckled my seat belt while he slid behind the wheel. He checked his phone before asking, "How about this new place I keep hearing about? It's a wine and coffee bar. It's supposed to be quiet. Dim lights."

"Oh, yeah, definitely."

He dropped his phone in a cupholder and pulled of his spot. "How was your OT appointment today?" I made an annoyed sound, and he laughed softly. "That bad?"

"Danny made me play *Perfection* again. It gives me a panic attack every time he takes it off the shelf."

"It gives everyone a panic attack. It's a terrible game." He turned out of the parking lot and onto the nearest street. "How were classes? You feel like you're getting all the support you need?"

"Kunal has organized everything for me. He put together a group of our classmates to help with notes and studying. His mom came over with him the other day and filled my freezer with enough food to feed an army. She even labeled the containers and made a little calendar to make sure I know which container to grab for each day."

"I've never met her, but she sounds like a really sweet lady."

"So sweet," I agreed. "She's so proud of Kunal for deciding

he's going to med school."

"Med school? Really?" He seemed to think it over. "I can see him as a doctor, but not a surgeon."

"He'll be a great doctor, whatever specialty he chooses," I insisted. "What about Hannah? Isn't she in some sort of biomedical science?"

"Tissue Engineering is her focus."

I made a face at the idea of spending day after day watching human tissue grow in petri dishes. Not wanting to get into the science of that, I asked, "How are things going between you?"

"We're taking it slow," he said, turning at an intersection. "We're going out tomorrow."

"Slow is good," I murmured, shifting my gaze out the window to the blur of passing headlights. "Things went fast with Hagen, and it blew up in my face."

Kyle's hand gently closed over mine. "I wish you didn't have to go through this. I know it must be painful."

I squeezed his hand back. "It is, but that's life, I guess."

"It seems so," he agreed, letting go of my hand as he eased to a stop at a red light. "Have you heard anything about Janine?"

"No, and I hope I never do."

"Don't you want her to pay for her crimes?"

"She can't go back in time and undo her attack. She lost Travis. She's suffered enough, and I'm not interested in vengeance. I just want to move on."

"You're a better person than me," he said after a moment.

"No," I disagreed. "I'm just tired of it all. I want to forget it ever happened. All of it."

Kyle reached for my hand again, and I welcomed his support and friendship. "I'm here to help you however I can. Whatever you need, just ask."

"Thank you. I really appreciate everything you've done for me."

He smiled at me and merged into the turn lane, dropping my hand so he could turn into the parking lot. We parked and got out of his car. My vision issues made me nervous and unsteady so I kept my gaze focused on the ground, trying to make sure i didn't stumble or trip. For a Thursday evening, there seemed to be quite a few people going in and out of the restaurants and coffee shop. I was grateful for Kyle's help as he steered me along.

Suddenly, he grabbed my arm and tugged hard, stopping me right in my tracks. I frowned at him and started to ask him what he was doing, but the expression on his face startled me. I followed his gaze, and my stomach dropped like a runaway elevator.

Hagen. Coming out of the coffee shop. And he wasn't alone.

It was my nurse. It was Vicky. His one-time ex.

God, she was so pretty. She looked effortlessly sexy in a deep navy dress that highlighted her incredible legs and curves. Seeing them side by side, his hand on the small of her back as he guided her out the door, I was struck by how perfect they seemed to fit together. It was like a knife to the gut as I realized how ridiculous we must have looked, him towering over tiny, skinny little me.

For a very brief and very weak moment, I silently willed him to see me. I wanted him to lock eyes with me, to let me see that he no longer loved me. A part of me, a pathetic and embarrassing part of me, wanted to shout his name, to ask him why he left me like that. How was it so easy to walk away from me? Why hadn't he fought for me?

I swallowed down the sob that threatened to escape and clung gratefully to Kyle's hand as he quickly turned us away from the coffee shop. Neither of us said a word as he hurried me back to his car and bundled me inside. He sat with his hands on the wheel as I cried silently next to him. The air conditioner blew across my wet cheeks, leaving my skin as cold as my broken heart.

"Should I take you home?" he asked gently.

"No, please, I don't want to be alone right now." I wiped at my face with the cuff of my hoodie. "I don't care where we go. Just not back to my apartment."

"Okay." He grabbed his phone and tapped at the screen. Eventually, he dropped his phone in the console and started to drive. I stared out the window, not really paying attention until he pulled into a Starbucks drive-thru. Somehow, he remembered my preferred drink—grande cinnamon dolce latte, breve, with no whipped cream and extra cinnamon sprinkles. The only other person to ever manage that was Hagen.

Hagen who had left me, wounded and afraid in a hospital, so he could date my nurse.

Not even the soothing warmth and sweetness of the latte could ease the throbbing ache inside me. Objectively, it wasn't hard to understand why he had sought out the company of an ex-girlfriend. She was familiar. She was kind and had a good heart, if her nursing care toward me was any indication.

My traitorous brain pointed out that Vicky was also settled in her life and had no plans to leave Houston. She matched Hagen's stage of life. She probably wanted the same things he did, the things I hadn't been able or ready to give him just yet. She was exactly the sort of partner he needed now. If not her, someone similar.

Kyle parked near the Waterwall, and I was pleasantly surprised by the destination he had chosen. It was quiet this time of night and the lights shining through the towering waterfall sculpture were relaxing. We found a bench close by the water and sat side by side, listening to the soothing sounds. I closed my eyes and inhaled deeply, glad to be outside in the cool evening and surrounded by the lulling noise of water.

Overcome with gratitude, I leaned my head on his shoulder. "Thank you for being such a good friend. I don't know what I would do without you, Kunal or Taylor."

He slid his arm around me and gave me a friendly squeeze. Or, at least, it started friendly.

His hand moved from my shoulder to my waist, grasping me and drawing me closer. Even with my double vision, I could see the look on his face wasn't one of friendship. No, it was something else. Something darker. Lustier.

"Kyle," I protested, desperate to avert the disaster waiting to happen.

"I know," he said, as if he understood something I didn't.

Before I could react, he quickly kissed me, his lips smashing into mine as I tried to pull back. He grabbed the back of my neck to hold me in place and stabbed his tongue against my lips. I pressed them together, refusing to let him taste me in that intimate way. He was too strong for me, and even though I resisted, I couldn't break free.

When his hand moved toward my still healing injury, I jolted at the sudden shock of pain. I gripped the coffee cup so hard it exploded all over us, scalding us both with the super-heated liquid inside. He howled in pain and jerked away from me. "Cassie! What the fuck?"

"What are you doing?" I scooted away from him, putting as much distance between us as possible without falling off the bench. I gingerly touched my head and glanced at my fingers, relieved not to see blood.

"I was following your lead."

"What lead?" I gawked at him as if he were a complete idiot. "What are you talking about?"

"Come on, Cassie! You don't have to keep playing these games, okay? Hagen is gone. You saw him earlier. He's moved on—and now it's time for you to do the same."

"With you?" I guessed, starting to feel so damn stupid. "You think I'm ready to rebound from the most serious relationship of my life in just a few weeks?"

"He was trash, Cassie. He was a lowlife scumbag loan shark. He was never going to be the right man for you. He was only ever going to hurt you." Kyle moved toward me again and grabbed my hands. "Cassie, you're so special. You need a man who will worship you."

My stomach lurched. "I don't want someone to worship me."

"That's because you don't know any better," he insisted in the most patronizing way. "You don't know how good I can be for you. I can show you if you'll let me. I'll spend hours in bed with you," he promised. "Touching you. Kissing you. Making love to you."

When he licked his lips, I almost hurled. "Kyle, we're friends. I don't...I don't see you *that* way, okay?"

His expression morphed instantly. His eyes blazed with anger. "Are you fucking serious right now with this friendzone bullshit? After everything I've done for you? After all the heartbreak I saved you from?"

"I thought you were my friend! That you were helping me because that's what friends do! We help each other!" My head was throbbing now, and I couldn't figure out when everything had gone so wrong. "What about Hannah? She's your girl-friend!"

"No, she isn't! We had one date, and she blocked me eve-rywhere. Stupid, stuck up cow!"

"Why did you lie about dating her?"

"Are you kidding me? All of you foids crave a man already in a relationship with another female. I knew I had to play your game to get you to see me as someone worthy of your attention."

"Foids? What does that even mean? And I don't want to date someone who is already in a relationship! I'm not into cheating!"

"Hagen is," he snarled cruelly. He tugged his phone out of his pocket, tapped the screen and then threw it at me. "Look at him. He didn't even make it three days after walking out on you before he was throwing money at whores."

I didn't want to look, but I couldn't stop myself. I covered my left eye so I could focus more easily and stared at the screen. The photos were dark, but the flash of neon stage lights illuminated Hagen's familiar profile well enough for me to recognize him. He was sitting next to well-known monster and strip club owner Besian Beciraj. He had his suit jacket off and his sleeves rolled up, showing off his muscular forearms. There was a glass of what I knew was his favorite bourbon sitting in front of him.

I hesitated before thumbing through the photos that followed. The women on the stage were gorgeous. Lush curves and sex appeal that I would never manage.

When I reached a photo of Hagen on a velvet sofa with a woman gyrating on his lap, I almost lost it. She was incredibly beautiful, and even though he wasn't touching her, he was still crossing the line. His expression was lazy and relaxed, one I had only seen once before when he had gotten drunk during a card game with Besian and some of their underworld friends.

Stamping down the humiliation washing over me in a burning wave, I threw the phone back at him. "Were you following Hagen?"

"I had to," Kyle insisted. "I knew you would want him back. You're weak, and you don't know what's best for you."

I gawked at him, wondering how I had been so blind. Taylor had been right along. He was Creeper Kyle. "You're a psycho."

"I'm a psycho? Well, I'd rather be a psycho than a little slut who spread her legs to pay off her brother's gambling debts!"

Swallowing hard, I tried to ignore the sting of his accusation. "Maybe I am a little slut, but I'll never be *your* little slut."

Refusing to spend another second in his presence, I grabbed my crumpled cup of coffee and left. I walked as fast as I could, ignoring Kyle as he yelled hurtful obscenities at me. When I couldn't hear him anymore, I stopped under a lamp post, threw my ruined cup in the trash and pulled my phone from the pocket of my hoodie. For a moment, I considered calling Taylor but she had already done so much to help me. I wasn't going to drag her into this shit show. Instead, I opened the Lyft app and managed to order a ride while covering my left eye.

The late model Kia Soul pulled up to the sidewalk where I had arranged to meet a few minutes later. Thankful the driver was a woman, I relaxed in the back seat and held it together through banal chitchat as she drove me home. When I finally made it inside my apartment, I locked the door and erupted in tears, sliding down the door in a crumpled heap of sadness and embarrassment.

My phone started to ring, and I ignored it, afraid that it was Kyle calling to harass me. When it rang the second time, I pulled it out of my hoodie and glanced at the screen. Even with double vision, there was no mistaking the smiling face of my brother. Desperate for someone I could trust, I answered the video call. "Ronnie!"

His smile faded instantly. "Cassie! What's wrong?"

"Ronnie, it's all ruined. It's all a mess. I don't know what to do anymore." Sobbing, I leaned back against the door and told him everything.

CHAPTER ELEVEN

L OUD KNOCKING AT the door to my apartment woke me. I rubbed my face and glanced at the clock by my bed. I had to cover my eye and squint to see the numbers correctly. It had been less than an hour since I had ended my long phone call with my brother. I must have only just fallen asleep.

As the knocking continued, a jolt of fear woke me up completely. What if it was Kyle?

Nervous and ready to call the police, I grabbed the first thing I could find to cover my naked body—my oversized hoodie that now smelled of coffee and cinnamon—and slipped it over my head. I held my phone tightly and slowly got out of bed, careful not to stand too quickly and fall. The wave of dizziness I experienced when standing upright faded faster than usual, and I took steady steps toward the front door, glad I had left the lights on when I fell asleep.

I was too short to see through the peep hole and didn't trust my balance for a stool or chair. Instead, I kept the chain in place, unlocked the deadbolt and opened the door only a few inches.

Hagen loomed in my doorway, his left hand braced on the frame and his right balled up to knock again. Seemingly startled by the door opening, he went from an expression of worry to one of utter relief. "Cassie."

Shocked at Hagen's unexpected appearance on my door-step, I tried to ignore the frisson of excited heat that raced through my body at the sound of my name falling from his lips. I stared up at him through the tiny space between the door and the frame. He looked like hell. His eyes were tired, and the lines around his face that crinkled when he smiled were deeper. His hair was a mess, as if he'd been running his fingers through it, and his usually immaculate clothing was wrinkled. "Hagen."

"Can I come inside? Please," he asked in a desperate way I had never heard him use.

After a moment's hesitation, I closed the door long enough to remove the chain. I opened it again, stepping aside so he could come into my apartment. Closing it, I leaned back against the door and gazed up at him. He made my cramped studio look even smaller. His head was inches from the ceiling fan, and I was glad I hadn't turned it on earlier. His arms were long enough that he could probably touch the far wall of the living area and the kitchen counter at the same time.

His gaze roamed over me, starting at my head and moving all the way down to my bare feet. I felt suddenly self-conscious in just my hoodie with nothing at all on underneath. Tugging at the hem of my hoodie, I asked, "What are you doing here?"

"I'm doing what I should have done weeks ago when I got that fucking message," he said roughly. I started to ask him what message he was talking about, but he gestured to the loveseat. "Can we sit? Talk?"

I nodded and skirted around him, not trusting myself to touch him again without breaking into a million little pieces.

"How did you know where to find me?"

"Ronnie," Hagen explained, taking the spot next me on the small couch. "He called and told me about what happened in the park tonight." Hagen wiped his hand down his face and sighed. "He made me realize what a colossal asshole and coward I've been."

I wasn't going to disagree with that. "Ronnie shouldn't have bothered you. I'm not your problem anymore."

Hagen grasped my hands between his and commanded my gaze. "You were *never* a problem to me."

The dam holding back my tears and emotions burst as the warmth of his hands flowed into mine. "You left me," I wept, unable to stop myself from showing how vulnerable and hurt I was. "You left me at the hospital, and you never came back."

"Cassie, baby," Hagen touched my face, "you told me not to come back. You told me it was over. You told me you never wanted to see me again, that you would never forgive me for what I took from you."

Still crying, I looked at him in confusion. "What are you talking about? I never sent you any messages like that." Tugging one of my hands free, I used the cuff of my hoodie to wipe my eyes. "You didn't answer any of my messages either."

"Cassie, I never got any other messages from you. Not after the break-up text," Hagen added. "You were very clear about how you felt and what you wanted done. You told me to send all your things to Kyle's place and—"

"John," I interrupted forcefully, "I never texted that to you. I couldn't have."

He shifted in his seat and retrieved his cell phone, unlocking the screen and opening his text messages. "Look."

I took the phone from him and hesitated before covering my left eye so I could focus on the screen.

"Cassie, is your eye still bothering you?" he asked softly and with worry.

I couldn't bear to look at him, to see the pity reflected in his face. Instead, I tried to make light of it. "Someone told me that I'd be cute in glasses."

"I'm pretty sure that someone said adorable," he corrected with a faint smile in his voice. "Is it…will it get better?"

"Maybe," I said, keeping my focus on the message in front of me. "I'll probably end up in special glasses at my next ophthalmology appointment. If that doesn't work, she wants to try surgery."

Hagen gripped my hand even tighter, and I could tell he was fighting the urge to haul me onto his lap. He kept that urge at bay and waited for me to read the text I had supposedly sent. It was a huge block of text filled with everything he had described—a definite end to our relationship and ugly, ugly words about how I would never forgive him.

"I didn't write this, Hagen." I handed the phone back to him. "I couldn't have. I can barely handle looking at any sort of screen right now. Back then? In the hospital?" I shook my head. "No way. Other than a short text I sent the morning after our fight, Taylor was the only one sending and answering messages on my phone. She wouldn't have sent that to you."

Wanting to prove it, I picked up my phone and opened my texts. "Here. Look for yourself."

Hagen did. "I never got these." He held his phone next to mine and compared the screens. Frowning, he said, "It's like we were having two different conversations. I wonder…"

As he tapped at both screens, I studied his face and breathed in the familiar smell of his cologne and aftershave. Just under the surface, I caught the scent of perfume, something sweet and heavy. It was a painful reminder of where he had been and that he hadn't been alone.

"Someone changed my number in your phone."

Drawn away from my troubled, jealous thoughts, I asked, "Who would do that?"

"Kyle," he growled. "That slimy piece of shit."

My stomach flip-flopped. "Oh my God. He had my phone the night I got hurt." My memories of that night were fuzzy but I remembered the important parts. The pieces all fit into place. "He lied to me about calling you and Ronnie. He wanted to be the only one with me at the hospital."

"I think it was more than that."

"What do you mean?"

He grimaced and rubbed the back of his neck. "I think he wanted me out of the way. He wanted you all for himself. After Ronnie called me and told me about the park, it all made sense." Scowling, he added, "I never trusted him. He had a vibe—a psycho stalker vibe—and I should have said something earlier. None of this would have happened."

A terrifying thought struck me. "Do you think Kyle attacked Travis?"

"Yes." He seemed to be warring with himself about something. Finally, he said, "One of my contacts sent me a message earlier tonight. There was a body found a few weeks ago. The face was all bashed in so it took a while to make the ID." He exhaled slowly. "It was Janine. They think she was killed the same night you ended up in the hospital. Maybe early the next morning."

"Kyle," I whispered, feeling certain that it was him. My blood ran cold as I considered how much danger I had unknowingly put myself in earlier. "What if I had been in his car when he made his move? When I rejected him?" I shuddered. "He had to let me walk away because there were witnesses at the park."

"Jesus, Cassie," Hagen said on a pained breath. In an instant, his arms were around me, and he hauled me closer, right up onto his lap. "I don't even want to think about what he would have done."

Fighting the desperate need to burrow into his familiar warmth, I pushed away from his chest and forced him to look at me. "I saw you tonight. With *her*. With Vicky."

He seemed taken aback. "At the coffee place?"

"Yes."

"Cassie, nothing happened. We met for a drink. We talked. She drove home in her car, and I went home in mine. Alone," he emphasized. "It wasn't serious."

"Like the lap dance?" I forced him to meet my gaze and instantly saw the shame and regret.

"I was drunk, but I can't blame it all on the alcohol. I should never have gone out with Besian and Kostya. I should have kept my dumb ass at home." He exhaled roughly. "I was hurting, and I wanted to stop feeling that way," he admitted. "I wanted to forget about our fight. I wanted to forget that look on your face right before I walked out like a coward."

"And did you forget?"

"No." He cupped my face in one big hand and held my gaze. "That whole night—the drinking, the dancers—it made me realize how much I had lost. It made me realize how much I loved you, but also how my actions—going after Travis and Janine like some alpha asshole—put you at risk. I didn't kill Travis, but I do carry some responsibility for what happened to you. If I had let it go, if I'd never confronted them in the laundry room, Janine never would have suspected me of hurting him. She never would have attacked you." He swallowed hard, and his eyes glimmered with guilty tears. "You were right, Cassie. It was my fault. I promised I would take care of you and protect you. I failed you. Completely."

Overcome with emotion, I pressed my forehead to his. Silent tears dropped down our cheeks. "I don't blame you."

"You should."

"But, I don't."

"I wish I could take it back—the strip club and coffee with Vicky. Even though nothing happened, it makes me feel like slime that I was that close to making the worst mistake of my life."

"You thought we were over," I reasoned, trying to be fair. Even though it had hurt me to see him at the strip club or with Vicky, I said, "It wasn't cheating if we were over."

Hagen stroked my cheek and seemed to be working up the courage to ask, "Are we over?"

"I don't want to be," I admitted tearfully.

"But?" Hagen studied my face, clearly afraid to hear my answer.

"But maybe this was for the best," I said in a painful rush. "I'll be leaving in a few months. I'll be in grad school for at least six years—maybe longer if I do post-grad research or find a job. Your whole life is here—your house, your businesses, your friends. I can't ask you to give all of that up for me."

"You don't have to ask, Cassie." His thumb caressed my jaw, and I leaned into his touch. "I was already planning to go with you."

"You were?"

"Why do you think I went out to California to meet with those investment firms? I wanted to meet with the fund managers, but I also scouted the housing situation near the campuses you were considering."

I was stunned. "Why didn't you say anything?"

"I wanted it to be a surprise. I planned to go with you on your grad school interviews and make a romantic getaway of it. Book a nice suite. Wine and dine you. Take you to see some houses so you could get an idea of where you wanted us to live."

I sagged against him, tucking my face into his neck. "I was so worried about moving away, and the whole time you were planning to come with me."

"Cassie," he murmured tenderly. His lips brushed my temple, and he held me tighter. "I'm so sorry. I should have said something sooner. I thought a surprise would be romantic."

"It would be," I assured him, lifting my head and kissing his jaw. "God, we've been so miserable. It could have all been avoided if we had just been brave enough to talk to each other."

"I know," he agreed, his voice thick with emotion. "I would change it all in a heartbeat if I could." He nuzzled his nose against mine. "You have to know, Cassie. Ever since you walked into my bar, you've been the only thing that matters to me. You have my whole fucking heart. All of it. It's yours." He brushed his lips gently against mine. "Can we start over? Or pick up where we left off in the hospital?"

"Yes." I kissed him, pressing our lips together and savoring the familiar heat of him. "I mean, technically, we never actually broke up. It was all Kyle manipulating us."

"That motherfu—," he cut off before finishing the word. "Don't worry about him. He's going to get what he deserves."

I fixed him in place with a chastising look. "What happened to not going full alpha?"

"I'm going to call in a favor. It's not alpha if you outsource."

I decided not to ask which of his questionable friends owed that favor. "A favor that puts him in jail? Where he belongs? Not tossed into the Gulf with cement shoes?"

"Cement shoes? What is this? Miami? 1988?" Hagen laughed that dark, rich laugh that I had missed so much. "No. I'll make sure he ends up in jail."

Toying with the collar of his shirt, I asked, "Do you think he's tracking your phone? Or your vehicle? Or both?"

"Yes. Both," he growled. "It wouldn't surprise me if he took you to that coffee shop earlier tonight on purpose. Vicky asked me to meet her through a text. Maybe he's reading them."

"He looked at his phone before we left the parking lot. He must have been checking to make sure you were there." I made a face. "Taylor is going to be impossible once she finds out he really is a creep. She's been telling me forever that he's a 'nice guy' type. I should have listened to her."

"Your heart is so big and gentle. You always see the best in people. It's one of the things I love about you. You're always so optimistic and positive. It never occurs to you that people are devious dirtbags."

"I guess I am a little naïve," I allowed.

Hagen kissed me. "There's nothing wrong with that. It's what makes you so good. It's why people love you and want to be your friend. Your big, soft heart has enough love for everyone who needs it." He captured my mouth and gently cupped my nape. "I need it. I need you. You have to know that your love has made me a better man."

Seeing the truth in his eyes, I nodded. "I love you."

"I love you." He smiled warmly. "Come home with me?"

"Yes." Letting him pick me up, I rested my head right in the crook of his neck where it fit perfectly and seemed to belong. Home with Hagen was exactly where I wanted to be.

CHAPTER TWELVE

"YOU HUNGRY?" HAGEN asked as he pulled out of the parking lot of the apartment complex. "I can stop somewhere before we get home."

Ever since Hagen had arrived on my doorstep, the nauseating knot in the pit of my stomach that had been tormenting me for weeks began to dissipate. It was as if his presence and his apology had soothed away the anxiety. Had my body been trying to tell me that something wasn't quite right with the situation? Was it my subconscious rebelling against the idea that Hagen would just leave me and not come back?

Hungry for the first time in days, I admitted, "I'm starving."

"We can't have that." He grasped my hand and rubbed his thumb over the back of it. "Whataburger?"

"Oh my gosh," I said with a little groan. "That sounds so good!"

My mouth was watering by the time we pulled into the drive-thru, and I didn't even try to wait until we got back to his place to eat. I nibbled on the crispy fries and enjoyed the giant Dr. Pepper as Hagen navigated his SUV through the late-night traffic.

He seemed pensive as he drove, and I waited for him to

say whatever it was that was bothering him. Eventually, he asked, "Cassie?"

"Yeah?"

"I know how much it took for you to forgive me tonight, for you to agree to let me back into your life." He glanced at me so I could see his serious expression. "I'll do whatever I can to regain your trust."

"Just be you," I said, reaching out to take his hand. "What we went through wasn't totally on either of us. We were manipulated by a psycho. Yes, one of us or both of us should have made an effort to track down the other and talk in person. That was our mistake. The rest of it?" I shook my head. "That's on Kyle."

"I agree, but I want to make sure that you know that I'm not expecting things to go right back to the way they were. I know you might need some time to get to the point where you trust me enough for us to be intimate or for you to want to move in with me again."

"I sublet that apartment from a grad student Taylor knows," I explained. "I can't move out and leave him hanging."

"If you decide you want to move in with me, I'll take care of the sublet rent. It's the least I can do after this whole mess."

"I'll think about it." I wasn't quite ready to jump back in with both feet. Having my own place to retreat to felt like a necessary safety net. "And, anyway, I can't drive so I need to be close to the METRO so I can get to class and therapy."

"I'm more than happy to be your chauffeur, Cassie."

"You have a life and businesses to run."

"You're the only business that matters, and my life was

shit without you." He squeezed my hand. "I mean it, Cassie. Whatever I have to do to earn back your trust, I'll do it. Anything. Just ask, and I'll make it happen."

"John," I murmured, thinking it wouldn't take much.

"Anything," he repeated as he turned into his neighborhood.

Wanting to tease him and lighten the serious mood just a little, I asked, "Anything like, oh, Iceland? Golden Circle? Northern Lights?"

"I'll book the flights to Reykjavik in the morning."

I laughed softly. "I can't fly for a few more weeks."

"When you're ready, you let me know."

I had been joking, but he was absolutely serious about taking me to Iceland. It had always been a bucket list trip for me, and the idea of sharing it with Hagen, of cuddling together under the night sky to watch the vibrant glow of the aurora borealis filled me with a happy warmth.

When we pulled into Hagen's driveway, there was a black Audi parked in front of the house. I glanced at Hagen, and he said, "I sent Kostya a text while you were packing your bag."

"Your favor?"

He nodded and pulled into the garage. "I've been keeping that one in my back pocket a long time."

"I'm sorry you have to use it on this."

"I'm not." He lifted my hand and kissed the back of it. "I'd pay whatever price he asked to keep you safe."

And he would. Of that, I was absolutely certain.

Once we made it inside, Hagen went to the front door to let Kostya in and I took a seat at the breakfast nook. He returned with the intimidating Russian trailing behind him. I warily watched Kostya as he placed a sinister black leather bag on the island. There was something about him, something in his eyes and the way he moved, that struck fear in me. He seemed secretive and dangerous, and I wasn't sure I ever wanted Hagen to owe him a favor.

Kostya didn't bother with small talk. "What did Kyle have access to while you were in the hospital?"

Not wanting to irritate him by taking too long to answer, I quickly said, "My backpack, car, apartment, phone and laptop. He had my keys so he could have gotten into all of my stuff."

"That backpack?" Kostya gestured to the bag Hagen had carried in for me.

"Yes."

"May I?"

"Of course."

While he took my backpack to the nearby island, I ate quietly at the table and watched him work. Hagen sat next to me, his gaze never leaving Kostya and his hand resting comfortingly on my thigh. The Russian went through my backpack, taking everything out and placing it on the marble counter. He retrieved a small device from the black bag he had brought with him and used it to scan my phone and laptop. He frowned and then waved the device over my backpack.

My eyes widened when he set aside the device and whipped out a knife. Before I could tell him not to cut my backpack, he flicked his wrist in a practiced motion that had the knife's blade sliding out and made a slit in the lining of the smallest front pocket. He used the tip of the blade to poke around and finally found something. He held up a thin black rectangle. "This is an active GPS tracker."

Suddenly, slicing open my backpack didn't seem like such a big deal. "Oh my God. How long has that been in there?"

"Hard to say," Kostya replied as he studied the device. "The battery on this might last a week." He examined my backpack more closely. "I think he's probably been putting a tracker on you for a long time. There are small, mended slits here and here…and here." He pointed them out to us and then scratched at the fabric in a few spots. "Superglue."

Feeling violated, I asked, "If he's been following me with a GPS tracker, could he have been watching me in other ways? Like cameras in my apartment?"

"It's possible." Kostya set down the tracker. "I'll need to take your phone and laptop with me to my tech person."

"We'll get a new phone and laptop tomorrow," Hagen interjected, his jaw tight and his voice hard. "I don't want anything that asshole touched near you ever again."

"My tech can transfer everything onto your new devices. She runs a security firm so she has laptops and phones in stock. She can give you something similar or better than what you have now."

"Yes. Have her do that," Hagen decided.

"I'll make sure you get the new ones back in the morning." He glanced toward the garage. "Your SUV unlocked?"

"No." Hagen got up and kissed the top of my head before taking Kostya out to the garage.

Alone in the kitchen, I finished my last few bites and threw away my trash. When I was done, I stared at my backpack, wondering what in the hell possessed Kyle to do something so bizarre and violating. Why hadn't I been able to see that he wasn't my real friend? Was I the only woman he had done this to or were there others?

Kostya and Hagen walked back into the kitchen a few minutes later. Kostya had another GPS tracking device in his hand. He tossed it into his black bag along with the other tracker, my phone and laptop. He touched the keys he had taken out of my backpack earlier. "Are these to your apartment and car?"

"Yes."

"What's the address?" After I gave it to him, he nodded and turned his attention to Hagen. "Do you want me to sweep your businesses?"

"Can't hurt," Hagen replied.

"I'll get on it tomorrow." Kostya picked up his bag. "I'll text you with any updates."

"Thank you," Hagen said and walked Kostya to the front door. When he came back, he held out his hand, and I gratefully went to him, melting into his warm embrace. He pressed his lips to the top of my head again. "I'm sorry this has happened to you."

"I'm sorry you got dragged into it."

"I'm not. I'm glad you're not trying to handle this alone." His big hand rubbed my back, and I relaxed under his touch. "You ready for bed?"

Realizing just how late it was, I nodded. "Do you mind if I shower first?"

"Do you mind if I join you?" He stroked my face. "No expectations," he added hastily. "I'm not trying to—"

"I know," I interrupted, turning my head to kiss his palm. This close to him, warmed by his body heat and surrounded by his scent, I began to feel the stirrings of desire low in my belly. "You can have expectations tomorrow."

The corners of his mouth lifted in a grin. "Great expectations?"

I groaned at his horrible pun. "It's been a while so I'm rusty. Let's go with lowered expectations."

He laughed and lowered his mouth to mine. Hand in hand, we moved through the house, turning off lights and checking the doors. He carried my small suitcase upstairs and helped me unpack it before leading me to the upholstered bench at the end of the bed. He sat and beckoned me closer.

As if unwrapping a gift, he took his time peeling away my clothing. When I was naked, he let his hands settle on my waist. Even sitting, he was taller than me, but it was easier to stare into each other's eyes this way. He leaned forward and began dotting featherlight kisses along my hairline and down each cheek before gently pressing his lips to the tip of my nose and then my mouth. His kisses traveled lower, dusting my jaw and neck and then even lower to the swell of each breast.

With his forehead resting against my chest, he exhaled roughly and confessed, "I was fucking lost without you."

I slid my arms around his broad shoulders and hugged him close. The hands on my waist moved toward my hips and then to my bottom. Grasping me with both strong hands, he lifted me into his lap and I wrapped my legs around him, savoring the closeness we had been denied for so many weeks.

"I'm here now." I kissed his temple and combed my fingers through his short hair. "It will take more than Kyle to send me away again."

His arms tightened around me. "I want to throttle him. I want to make him hurt." He nuzzled into my neck. "But I won't. I won't risk losing you again."

Knowing how hard it was for him to take a step back and not go after Kyle in the way he wanted, I held his face between my smaller hands and tenderly kissed him. "I love you, John."

"I don't deserve it," he whispered against my lips, "but I'll do whatever I can to keep it."

He sealed his vow with a loving kiss before tucking a few stands of loose hair behind my ear. Believing he would, I reached for the top button of his shirt. What should have been an easy task wasn't so simple anymore, but I took my time and managed all of them. When I glanced at Hagen expecting to see pity, I only saw encouragement.

I pushed the shirt off his shoulders, and he shrugged out of it before standing to rid himself of the rest of his clothing. Once we were both naked, he took my hand, and I followed him into the bathroom. He turned on the shower and kept hold of my hand when I stepped in after him, as if he knew I would be unsteady on my feet.

With movements that were almost reverent, he washed my body and carefully shampooed my hair. He hesitated when his fingers neared my still healing scar. "I don't want to hurt you."

"You won't." I glanced back at him over my shoulder. "Just don't touch the center of it. It's kind of soft, and it feels weird."

"Duly noted." He took his time, cautiously skirting the edges of the wound as he washed and conditioned my hair. When he was done, I thanked him and kissed his chest before leaning back against the tile wall for support. I enjoyed the view, watching the suds rush down his incredible body and swirl around his feet.

After we were both clean, we stepped out onto the bath mats. He wrapped a towel low around his hips before taking a fluffy towel in hand to dry me. I could have done it myself, and it would have been faster, but there was something so incredibly beautiful about the silent apology he was making to me. His actions tonight were his way of showing me that he was serious about doing whatever it took to earn back my trust. He was serious about taking care of me and being there for me. He wanted to atone for his mistakes, and I let him, relishing the feel of his hands gently drying my hair.

As we stood side-by-side at the double vanity brushing our teeth, it was if we had never been apart. Watching him in the mirror, realizing how much we had missed each other and how close we came to never reuniting, I was suddenly gripped with anger at Kyle. If we were right in suspecting he had been the one behind the fatal attack on Travis, he had been the cause of my injury. He had tried to take everything from me— my life, my sight, my education, my future career and my life with Hagen. Somehow, some way, he would pay for what he had done to all of us.

"You look mad as hell," Hagen remarked as I adjusted the pillows to an angle that would help keep my head lifted and comfortable.

"Not at you," I assured him as he snuggled in close, wrapping his arms around me and resting his head against my chest. I reveled in the heat of his bare skin on mine, of his lips brushing against my throat and his fingertips trailing down my arm.

"What time do you need to be on campus?"

"I'm not going to campus in the morning. I have a neuro

appointment."

"Can I come with you?"

"Yes." I ran my fingers through his still damp hair. Feeling sleepy and relaxed, I yawned and let my eyes close. Exhaustion took its toll, but I felt so safe with Hagen that I didn't mind. I was finally right back where I belonged.

CHAPTER THIRTEEN

"YOU WANT ME to walk you into the building?" Hagen asked as he pulled to the curb and parked.

"I can handle it," I assured him, reaching out to adjust my new glasses. After my neuro appointment on Friday morning, I had been sent to see the ophthalmologist for special lenses to help with my double vision. I had spent the weekend getting used to them but still had moments where I stumbled or lost my balance.

"If you get a headache, call me."

"I will." I grabbed my new backpack from the floorboard and slid my arms through the straps.

"And if you need anything, call me."

"Okay," I promised with laugh. He was almost too over-protective since we had gotten back together. Almost.

"And if you see Kyle—"

"Mace and brass knuckles?"

He frowned. "Please tell me that you are joking and that crazy Fox girl didn't set you up with those."

Fox was the security tech Kostya had introduced us to the morning after his late-night visit. She owned a local security company that focused on women's security needs and had been very helpful. She was a bit quirky, though, and Hagen hadn't been sold on her as quickly as I was.

"No, she didn't." I leaned over and pecked his cheek. "But Taylor did!"

"Cassie!" He called after me as I escaped the SUV with a grin and a laugh. "Be careful!"

"I will be."

"Love you."

"Love you, too," I said before closing the door and stepping onto the sidewalk. I returned his wave before hiking my backpack a little higher on my shoulders. Replacing my old and well-loved bag had been easier once I had become aware that Kyle had been hiding tracking devices in it. I had put it away in a box, not quite ready to throw it away just yet.

"Hey, Cass," Kunal greeted as I took the seat next to him. He grinned mischievously and said, "I like the glasses. Very Hillary Clinton circa 2013."

I snorted. "Wow. Thanks? I guess."

He laughed and clicked his pen a few times. "Do they help?"

"Immensely." I opened my notebook and picked out the green pen I preferred for my class notes. "I can actually read text on paper, and my peripheral vision is a lot better."

"What about screens? Can you use your phone? Laptop?"

"For short bursts of time," I confirmed with a nod. "I think it will get better the more I practice."

Our professor walked in, and the discussions around the room faded to nothing. When the lecture started, I felt absolute relief at being able to see and read the whiteboard and my own notes. For the first time in weeks, I was able to follow a lecture without feeling lost and take notes that were legible.

By the time class ended, I could feel my confidence starting to rebuild.

"Did you see the front page of the *Thresher* today?" Kunal asked as we packed up our things.

I shook my head. "I haven't read the paper in weeks."

"You should check it out. It's an in-depth report on the missing students." He made a face. "It doesn't paint the administration or the police in a very good light."

"They probably deserve it. It's been years and none of them have been found."

He made an agreeing sound as we walked out of the classroom. "How are you set on meals? Mom wanted me to ask if you need another delivery."

"I'm good, but I'll be sure to let you know when I get low." I smiled at him. "How are my notes from last semester working out for you?"

"They're great. Exactly what I needed," he assured me. "You want me to walk with you to the Taylor and Minnie's lab?"

"No, I think I'm good today." I gestured to my glasses. "Thanks for offering, though."

"Anytime." He smiled before heading off in a different direction.

Mindful of the sidewalk cracks, I enjoyed my unhurried walk to the lab where Taylor and Minnie were running their neuro research project. It was strange being on the other side of the research equation but also enjoyable to see the progress I was making with my memory recall.

When I reached the lab, the door was closed with the privacy sign turned out toward the hall. Knowing that was Minh's way of keeping their participants protected, I took a seat in one of the chairs down the hall and waited for my turn. Remembering Kunal's comment about the school paper, I retrieved my phone from the thigh pocket of my leggings and navigated to the site.

The entire front page was dedicated to the missing students. There were long stories on each one of them as well as timelines of their last days before disappearing and interviews with their families and friends. One detail stuck out to me. All of the students had used the on campus counseling center.

Even with my glasses, I had to take breaks from staring at the screen. I had just glanced back and started to scroll to the story about Anna, a freshman and international student from Russia, when my gaze fell on a sickeningly familiar piece of jewelry.

There on her wrist, clear and bright and easy to recognize, was a blue enamel bead bracelet. I pinched the screen and zoomed in to the bracelet, looking carefully at the beads to be sure. One of the beads had a small defect, a little nick near the center of a black dot. Just like the bracelet Kyle gifted me.

It wasn't just a similar bracelet.

It was *the* bracelet.

My heart raced, and my stomach swirled. Was it possible? Was Kyle the person responsible for the disappearances of all these women? Had he met them at the counseling center where he volunteered? Had he picked them because they were struggling and desperate for friendship and help?

The details of the case, his odd behavior and the bracelet left no doubt. He was the monster who had done something terrible to these women. Was that what he had planned for me? To separate me from Hagen and make me weak and vulnerable so he could strike?

Thinking of Travis and Janine, the collateral damage in Kyle's twisted plan, made me absolutely sick. Who else had he hurt? What would happen when the police started following the trail of clues? Would they find things even worse than kidnapping and murder?

Panicked, I shot up out of the chair and grabbed my backpack. For a second, I considered busting in on the research session for Taylor's help, but I remembered that there was a campus police outpost not far from here. There was always a bike cop hanging around, ready to help if needed. I didn't bother waiting for the elevator to take me down to the ground floor. I used the stairs instead, my mind racing as I moved as quickly but cautiously as possible.

When I stepped out of the building, I dialed Hagen's number and cursed when it went to voicemail. "John, it's me. Please call me back as soon as you can. Come back to campus. I need you. It's about Kyle. He's the one who took those girls. I can prove it. The bracelet he—"

I gasped as a hand gripped my backpack and dragged me backwards into a bit of overgrown trees and shrubs that hugged the edge of the building. A hand slapped over my mouth, quieting me and making it impossible for me to call for help.

"Sorry, sweetheart, but your loan shark isn't going to save you this time," Kyle whispered harshly against my ear. He tugged the phone out of my hand and carelessly threw it behind him. "Those nosy fucking amateurs at the *Thrasher* just had to run that story today. I knew you'd get spooked, knew I had to get to you as quickly as possible. It was supposed to be easier than this. Gentler," he added before burying his face in my neck. He breathed in deeply, and I shuddered with disgust. "You're my special girl. I was mad at you after the park. I wanted to hurt you, but I've changed my mind," he explained magnanimously. "I'm going to take you to my special place and worship you."

It was clear that his idea of worship meant something terrible. I struggled to get free, and he hissed, "Don't fight me, Cassie."

Like hell was I going to listen this psycho! I threw back my elbow but missed. His hand moved to my neck, his fingers cruelly biting into my skin as he started to squeeze. Unable to shove him away with my elbows, I used my feet instead, stomping on his toes as hard as I could. He grunted in pain and loosened up just enough for me to get one arm out of my backpack straps.

"You fucking psycho creep!" Screaming like a banshee, I swung my backpack and walloped him right upside the head. "Help! Help me!"

Kyle rushed toward me, his eyes wild and desperate, but I was done being a victim. I wasn't going to let anyone else hurt me. Never fucking again.

I swung at him again, enjoying the thud of the backpack slamming into his ribcage. I screamed for help while battering him with the bag and kicking out at him. He managed to grab my ankle before I could connect with his calf and yanked hard enough to make me lose my balance.

As I tumbled back toward the ground, I could hear people yelling and coming closer. Kyle seemed to finally realize he had lost the element of surprise. He was out in the open now, and everyone would know his secrets.

He turned to run—and slammed right into Hagen's powerful fist. Breathing hard, jaw tensed, his suit jacket missing, Hagen gripped the front of Kyle's shirt and hauled him up off the ground. Kyle's feet dangled as Hagen shook him like a ragdoll before backhanding him and throwing him down in a bloodied, dazed heap.

Stepping away from Kyle who cried pathetically, Hagen strode toward me. He crouched down and cupped my face, surveying me for injuries. His thumbs traced the apples of my cheeks. "Are you okay? Did that piece of shit hurt you?"

"I'm okay." I grasped his thick wrists and held on tight. "How did you find me so fast?"

"Kostya called me. He told me he found something terrible and that I needed to get to you as fast as possible." He glanced back and scowled at Kyle who was now surrounded and detained by my fellow students. "I knew you were supposed to be at the research lab with Taylor. I ran here as fast as I could."

"John," I exhaled his name with relief and closed my eyes.

He kissed my forehead. "Can you stand?"

"Help me?"

He gently guided me to my feet and wrapped his arm around my shoulders, drawing me in close to his side. The campus police had arrived on the scene and were hauling Kyle to his feet as the onlookers excitedly described what they had witnessed. Kyle's face oozed blood, and as I stared at him, I tried to figure out how I had been so blind as to what a monster he was. The memory of Taylor comparing him to Ted Bundy filtered through, and I realized how right she was.

"Cass! What the hell happened?" Taylor rushed toward me and grabbed my hand. She looked at Kyle and then back at me. Triumphantly smug, she smirked. "What did I say? Fucking Ted Bundy, huh?"

I didn't know whether to laugh or cry. She seemed to know I was overwhelmed, and she hugged me tightly. "God, I was so worried! You weren't in the hallway, and I panicked. Kunal is on his way, too. I sent him a message to see if you had been in class."

Right as one of the police officers came forward to question me, Kunal appeared, panting and sweating from his mad dash across campus. With Hagen's hand on my lower back and Taylor and Kunal at my side, I inhaled a steadying a breath and prepared to tell the police everything.

CHAPTER FOURTEEN

THE MOST WONDERFUL sensation woke me. I stretched my arms overhead and smiled at the ticklish touch of Hagen's lips on my inner thigh. Of all the ways to be woken up by the man I loved, this was right at the top of the list.

The fireplace cast a soft glow around his bedroom. The heavy drapes were still pulled tightly together, blocking out the chill of a wintry morning and the too bright sun. His hands moved over my outer thighs and along my hips before sliding to my lower belly. He nuzzled closer and closer to where I wanted him most, taking his time and dragging out the anticipation.

"Hagen," I pleaded, my voice rough with sleep.

He decided to be merciful and dragged his tongue through my folds. I arched off the bed at the decadent contact and let my legs fall open even wider. He started slow and easy, exploring me with his tongue while his hands stroked my belly and breasts. When he drew my clit between his lips, he lightly pinched my nipple, and I gasped at the incredible burst of sharp pleasure and quicksilver pain. Knowing I would come apart, he worked his tongue against me while continuing to tug my nipples and knead my breasts.

Unable to do anything but feel, I gripped the sheets in

both hands and rocked my hips, pressing my pussy against his mouth for even more stimulation. I lifted my head and watched him feast on me. He made little pleasurable sounds, and when he opened his eyes to meet my gaze, I lost it. I came hard on a sharply inhaled breath. My thighs quivered as my hips undulated in time with the stroke of his tongue. "John!"

When my orgasm faded away, I dropped down to the bed, relaxed and panting. Hagen slid two of his fingers against my lips before dipping them into my mouth. I answered his silent command and licked them until they were wet and slick. Even knowing what was coming, I still moaned and shuddered when he thrust them into me. I cried out and fought the urge to close my legs against the onslaught of sensual torture that was sure to follow.

"Fuck, Cassie, I could eat your pussy all day and night and still want it again the next day." His growled filthy words made my stomach wobble. As if to prove he meant it, he used his thumb and finger to hold my labia apart, baring my clit to his attention. He was relentless as he traced and suckled the little pearl. His fingers thrust into me, searching and seeking until they found that spongy area along the front wall that made me scream.

"John!" I was shaking now, my whole body revving up for an orgasm that was going to leave me dizzy and breathless. There was a moment of fear as the pleasurable feelings built higher and higher. His tongue swirled, and his fingers stroked in just the right way. I came with a scream, and he went wild, using his shoulders to keep my legs open while he did wicked things with mouth, forcing me into a third climax that left me so sensitive I desperately tried to escape him while pleading for mercy. "John! *Please*. No, no, no."

He eased off with gentle kisses all around my vulva and carefully pulled his fingers free. As I tried to catch my breath, he rested his head on my belly. I combed my fingers through is hair, scratching his scalp the way he loved best and tugged him up to my mouth for the kiss I craved. My taste and scent were all around us as our tongues tangled together.

The hard length of him pressed against my thigh, and I wiggled my bottom until we were finally in line. Clutching his shoulders, I urged him into me, lifting my hips and rubbing my slick heat along his shaft. He groaned and grabbed my ass, pulling me right where he wanted before sliding into me on a deliberate thrust.

There was nothing rushed or hurried about our lovemaking this morning. We took our time, moving together lazily. We stopped to kiss and caress, all while sharing secret smiles and soft words of love. Wrung out from the pleasure Hagen had given me with his mouth, I wasn't going to be able to come with him, but neither of us minded. It was enough for me to feel him like this, to hold onto his strong shoulders and take every stroke and thrust he gave me.

More than anything, I wanted to feel him let loose. I wanted to watch him fall apart, to take his pleasure from my body and feel the same joy he had given me. He didn't make me wait too long. His thrusts came faster and harder, and I grasped his ass, pulling him deeper into me while begging him to wreck me. He didn't even try to hold back. He slammed into me and rocked jerkily against me, his cock throbbing inside me.

Forehead to forehead, we stayed like that, exchanging kisses and smiling. When he finally pulled away from me, we both groaned and sought each other's warmth. I curled up next to him and kissed his chest. "I love you."

"I love you," he murmured and stroked my back. "There should be another word for what I feel. Something stronger, more serious."

"There probably is in another language." I drew my initials on his chest. "We could look it up later."

He smiled tenderly and kissed me. "Sure, baby."

The alarm on his bedside clock began to chime, and we both sighed at the intrusion of reality into our love nest. When he reached for it, I asked, "Are you working today?"

"No, it's a reminder."

"To tell me what an incredible girlfriend I am?" I teased and made him laugh.

"I don't need a reminder for that, Cass, but just in case you've forgotten, you are incredible." He captured and kissed my hand. His expression turned serious, and he rolled on his side to better hold my gaze. "You are incredible, Cassie. Everything you've survived this year. Everything you've overcome. You're amazing. You're the strongest person I know."

"John," I whispered, a little embarrassed by his praise.

"I mean it, Cassie." He caressed my face and nuzzled his mouth against mine in a sweet kiss. "Nothing can stop you. Not a head injury. Not that asshole lunatic Kyle. Nothing."

They hadn't stopped me, but they had tried. Sometimes I couldn't believe what I had gone through during the last few months. Even now, curled up in bed with Hagen, it was shocking to think that a few weeks ago, I couldn't even read a whiteboard or recall lectures. Hell, I had even managed to beat *Perfection* just after Thanksgiving!

I had made so much progress, but I would still continue seeing my therapists and exercising my brain, eyes and hands. Some of the deficits, especially my peripheral vision on the left side, would never be fully recovered, but I had high hopes about everything else. Maybe my life wasn't going to be as easy as it was before the attack, but I was ready for the challenges ahead of me.

"Are you sure you want to attend the sentencing in January?" Hagen brushed his fingers through my hair. "You don't have to go."

"I do." I didn't want to see Kyle ever again, but now, knowing the full extent of his crimes from the plea deal he had signed, I wanted to see him accept his punishment for the horrific things he had done.

After he was taken into custody on campus, the whole horrible truth had been revealed. Kyle had been the one who beat Travis to death in an attempt to frame Hagen, and he had been the one who murdered Janine after she confronted him about Travis's attack. A police raid on Kyle's apartment had uncovered shoes with Travis and Janine's blood on the laces and in the grooves of the soles. A baseball bat that he had attempted to clean still had the tiniest traces of brain matter embedded in the wood grain. The DNA tests had come confirmed it belonged to Travis.

But the horror hadn't ended there. The police discovered terabytes of hidden camera footage from bathrooms around campus as well as violent pornography and snuff films. There had been additional footage from my apartment, but Kostya had gotten his hands on it and destroyed it. Whatever Kyle had captured of my private life would never be seen by anyone else.

Kyle's sick need to keep small trinkets from his victims had been his downfall. The bracelet he had given me was just one of many treasures he had hoarded in a macabre shrine dedicated to all the girls and women he had hurt. And there were so many.

His criminal history went all the way back to his child-hood including an incident in first grade where he had hurt a kindergartner in a way that made my skin crawl. When he was in his early teens, he had gotten into trouble for masturbating in public places and peeping in windows. Once he was in high school, he had learned to hide his crimes and had discovered an entire disgusting and demented online world offering all the terrible films he could ever want. It had fueled something dark and broken inside him until he couldn't stop himself from acting on those compulsions.

All of those records had been sealed, allowing him to at-tend college without anyone knowing how dangerous he was. The first girl he had stalked and raped had been a classmate during his undergrad years. She hadn't been able to see his face, and there wasn't any DNA evidence so he had gotten away with it. The crime sated his unnatural desires for a while, but as he neared his graduation, the memories weren't enough to sustain him. He had struck again, choosing a naïve fresh-man who was easy to manipulate into drinking cocktails he had spiked with date rape drugs.

As a cover, he had perfected the art of being the nice guy. He was friendly and kind, protective and sweet. He had sought the volunteer position at the counseling center to learn how to work vulnerable or inexperienced young women. He learned how to choose the easiest victims, how to gain their trust until they were caught up in his web and completely at his mercy.

Kyle had confessed to kidnapping and killing all of the missing students. The death of the first one, Anna, the girl who had owned the bracelet, had been a mistake. While he was assaulting her, she had broken free of the gag he had shoved in her mouth and tried to scream. He had panicked and strangled her.

From that moment forward, he couldn't stop thinking about killing other women. He had used the counseling center as a hunting ground. He didn't bother with alcohol or drugs to make his victims pliable because he wanted them to fight back. He needed their fear. He craved it.

Even now, all these weeks later, I still shuddered when I thought about how close I had been to becoming another victim. That night in the park could have ended so badly. I didn't even want to think about where he would have thrown my body when he was done. In the gulf like some of his victims? In an abandoned tank battery like the others?

"He can't hurt anyone else ever again," Hagen said, as if reading my mind. "He's done. He's going to be locked up for the rest of his life. No parole. He'll be in prison until he dies of old age or someone shanks him in a shower."

"Hagen, you aren't…?" I couldn't even bring myself to say the words. He was connected to the underworld. How easy would it be for him to hire someone to kill Kyle inside prison?

"I don't have to," he answered matter-of-factly. "That girl? Anna? The Russian?"

I finally understood what he meant. "Oh."

"Yeah."

"Was she...? Was her family connected to people like Kostya?"

He shook his head. "No, but it doesn't matter. She was one of them. You can't kill a Russian in this city without ending up in the morgue."

"Unless you're another Russian," I guessed quietly.

He made a grunting sound of agreement. "They play by different rules. The crime families in the city," he added. "They have a different moral code, but it works."

Not wanting to talk about Kyle or the mafia any longer, I let Hagen tug me out of bed and into the shower. His soapy hands on my body grounded me in the here and now. All the horrible things that had happened were in the past. Today was a new and beautiful day.

"What's on the schedule?" Hagen plucked a dark blue Henley from his neatly organized drawer.

"I'm baking pies for tomorrow. You're brining the turkey and fireproofing the backyard since you're determined to use that fryer." I shot him an annoyed look and picked out a comfy oversized plaid shirt to go with my black camisole and leggings. He was so excited to drop a turkey in blazing hot peanut oil. I had seen too many *YouTube* videos of exploding turkeys and boiling oil fires to share his excitement.

"It will be fine," he promised, giving my bottom a little smack. "What else do we need to prep? Any side dishes?"

"Taylor and Danny are bringing the stuffing and the sweet potato casserole. I don't know what Kunal is bringing but whatever it is will be delicious."

Hagen handed me a pair of festive red and green fluffy socks with nonslip grips on the bottom. Even though my double vision had mostly resolved itself as my brain healed, I still had issues with my peripheral and had moments where my balance wasn't so great. With all the marble and hardwood in his place, he wasn't taking any chances that I would fall and had stocked up on barre and yoga socks for me.

"His mom should open a restaurant. I'd invest in it."

It was an interesting idea, and one I thought Kunal might find worth considering. He was still planning to attend medical school, but it might ease the burden he felt if his mother had a business of her own that could support her and his younger siblings. Then again, restaurants were notoriously hard to run and had high rates of failure.

Hagen sat next to me on the bed. He exchanged the socks in my hand for a poinsettia red envelope sealed with a gold star. Wondering where he had been hiding it, I frowned at him. "I thought we were waiting to exchange gifts until tomorrow morning."

"We are." He shifted and hauled my feet onto his lap. "This isn't a Christmas gift."

"A really early birthday gift?"

"No." He slid a sock onto my left foot. "Not an early anniversary gift either."

Curious, I peeled up the sticker sealing the envelope and withdrew the glossy pamphlets and plane tickets. When my gaze settled on the unmistakable green glow of the aurora borealis over the gorgeous Icelandic countryside, I gasped. "John!"

He grinned as he slipped the other sock on my right foot.

"I wanted to give you enough time to shop and pack."

I looked at the date on our plane tickets. "We're leaving in four days?"

"Surprise." He leaned forward and kissed me. "You. Me. Iceland. The Northern Lights. New Year's Eve."

"John," I whispered, overcome with emotion. I threw my arms around him and kissed him like my life depended on it. "You are so wonderfully perfect."

"No, I'm not, but every day I'm with you, I promise I'll try to be as close to perfect as I can." He dragged me onto his lap and slid his hand under my camisole to rub the bare skin of my back. Right before he kissed me again, the doorbell rang. He sighed and pressed his forehead to mine. "About that reminder that went off earlier…"

"Yeah?"

"It's your brother and his girlfriend."

I blinked. "Ronnie is here?"

"Yes."

"Downstairs?" Excitement rippled through me. It had been so long since I had last seen my brother and the thought of spending Christmas with him and his girlfriend brought tears to my eyes. "Hagen, you give the best presents."

He brushed his lips across mine. His hand stroked my back, and he admitted, "Right now, I'm wishing I had put them on a later flight. I want to keep you like this for a little bit longer. Preferably naked," he added as his hand drifted to my bottom and gave it a squeeze.

"Later," I promised as I kissed his cheek and wiggled on his lap, feeling the hard outline of his desire against my thigh.

"I might keep you in bed the entire time we're in Iceland."

"I might let you." I held his face between my hands and kissed him with all the love I had for him. "You can keep me wherever you like."

"Right here is good," he murmured, his gaze warm and tender.

As the doorbell rang a second time, I captured Hagen's mouth in a passionate kiss. After everything we had been through, I was exactly where I was always meant to be, wrapped up in the arms of the loan shark who had changed my life in the most unexpected and wonderful ways.

The End

Also by Roxie Rivera

About the Author

A New York Times and USA Today bestselling author, I like to write super sexy romances and scorching hot erotica. I live in Texas on five acres with my husband, two daughters and our wild and ever-expanding menagerie of pets.

You can find me online at www.roxierivera.com.